ALWAYS A BRIDESMAID

Whiskey Ridge (Book 4)

CHAPTER 1

S amantha Ryan hated stereotypes. It was one of the things she worked on in her law practice every single day. Cases against corporations that discriminated in some way against one of her clients. Whether it was race, sexual orientation or gender, she fought - and won - most of her cases because of her ability to eloquently debate their side of the argument.

But today all she could hear in her head was the age old stereotype of "always the bridesmaid, never the bride".

She wished it didn't matter that she wasn't married in her mid-thirties. She wished that she wasn't so incredibly jealous that her younger sister had found the love of her life and was about to have the most amazing wedding in the north Georgia mountains. She wished that she could pluck out that jealous bone in her body that seemed to be wedged behind her ribcage, tweaking every heartbeat.

But here she was, sitting behind her fancy mahogany desk, staring out over the Atlanta skyline from the 20th floor of her luxury office building… thinking about how she was envious of her sister, Katie's, good fortune.

Samantha's life had always revolved around her career. Even when she was a little girl, her father - also an attorney - had drilled into her head that she was destined for law school. He'd said he saw the "gift" in her even when she was six years old and would hold mock court sessions with her stuffed animals. She vividly remembered looking through his thick legal books and wondering what it all meant, the smell of the musty paper assaulting her senses.

She'd followed directly in his footsteps, even attending his alma mater, The University of Georgia, and graduating with honors. When he'd died during her second year of law school, the ground seemed to give way beneath her feet. But she'd carried on, knowing that was what he wanted for her.

Meanwhile, her little sister was just about the

complete opposite. Katie was a free spirit, to say the least. She'd skipped college, opting instead to do volunteer work in the poorest areas of Central America for two years. Once she returned stateside, she got her license to become an esthetician and spent her days giving facials and spa treatments to women in some tiny mountain town called Whiskey Ridge.

So why was Samantha envious? She made more money in a month than most people made in a year. She had one of the fanciest, most expensive apartments in the whole city. She drove a brand new car every year. She even had a personal chef prepare her meals and deliver them every few days. Her life was what other people dreamed of.

But she was starting to feel empty. Even winning the big cases wasn't bringing her joy lately.

It had started with her mother's death five years ago. Watching her fade away after the cancer diagnosis had been heart shattering. But more than that, it'd made Samantha reevaluate her own life. What was she doing all this for? The long nights, the early mornings... what was the end goal?

At her mother's funeral, she suddenly realized that her life had no real purpose. Making money without a purpose was futile, in her opinion. Even at the funeral, she found herself longing for the kinds of connections she saw in family and friends. When the sad event was over, they all hugged and piled into cars together. She'd climbed into her small sports car and drove back to a lonely apartment.

So she'd started dating with the same vigor she'd had while pursuing her law degree, figuring that snagging a husband was just another task on her list. She'd find the right one, start her own family and she'd have an instant purpose in her life.

She hired an expensive matchmaker and went out on over a dozen dates before meeting Philip. He was a nice guy and very wealthy with his venture capital business. But after a few months, what little fire they had between them had burned out completely. In truth, it'd been like dating her brother, if she'd had one.

Deciding she couldn't force love and chemistry, she'd started hitting the bar scene, singles groups and borrowing shelter dogs from the Humane Society to walk around the park. At times, she felt ridiculous and desperate, but she continued until she met Clint.

They had chemistry. They hit it off immediately, and she really thought he was "the one". She'd even started planning what her wedding dinner would feature (filet mignon and pan seared tuna with a mango chutney). She recalled this time in her life as when she still had hope that Mr. Right was out there, that someone was the perfect match for her.

But then Clint found chemistry with an old high school girlfriend, and poof! He was gone too.

And then there was Clark, but she didn't like to think about him. Her relationship with him was the one major failure of her life.

Samantha sighed as she looked down at her desk. She picked up Katie and Rick's wedding invitation and ran her finger across the simple white ribbon that was woven through the thick card stock paper.

Katie had relocated to Whiskey Ridge years ago, calling it her perfect little mountain oasis. She'd met Rick there just after moving, and they'd had a storybook romance amidst the Blue Ridge Mountains.

Samantha had honestly been surprised when her sister asked her to be her maid of honor. It wasn't that they weren't close, but Katie certainly had good friends she'd assumed would be chosen for the role.

But her mother and father would want her to do this. She was all Katie had left of her family, and that meant the responsibility to make sure her sister had a great start to her marriage was all hers.

As an esthetician, Katie wasn't exactly rich. And

Rick ran a motorcycle repair shop, which Samantha thought was good money but it certainly wasn't enough to have a big fancy wedding in the city. Actually, Katie hadn't wanted that anyway, even when Samantha had offered. She wanted a small, country wedding at a little white chapel nestled under the blue tinged mountains.

Samantha had offered to pay for much of the wedding, but Rick and Katie had said no but thank you. They were good, hard working people, and Samantha's money wasn't something they wanted. They just wanted to be married and start their family.

Still, Samantha had wanted to do something big for her sister, especially since her parents weren't there. So, she'd splurged on an amazing honeymoon package that would take them all over Europe. They would eat baguettes in Paris under the shade of the Eiffel Tower and then drink tea like members of the Royal Family in London. She wanted her sister to have an amazing, month long dream honeymoon before she started her life as a wife.

"When is it my turn?" Samantha heard herself whisper as she ran the ribbon through her fingers one more time before putting the invitation into her drawer.

"What'd you say?" Eileen, her assistant, sauntered into her office and sat down. She wasn't the best assistant, but she walked around the office like it was her own personal runway anyhow.

"Nothing. Just mumbling. Did you file the Easton papers?" Samantha was almost always focused on business, especially when her emotions started to run away with her.

"Of course, Boss."

"Stop calling me that," she muttered as she looked for another file on her desk. "What about the company... the one that makes the coffee drinks..."

"Dayton Industries?"

"Right. Did Scott call about filing the appeal on that one?"

"Yes, Sam. Everything is under control. Why are you even still here?"

Samantha sighed. "You know I don't give up control easily."

"I know. I've worked for you for six years now, and this is the first vacation I've seen you take."

Samantha slid more files around on her desk. "It's not a vacation. I'm simply going to the mountains to make sure my baby sister has a great bridal shower, bachelorette party and wedding. Then I'm housesitting for a month." She sat stone faced, staring at Eileen.

"And you look thrilled about it," Eileen said with a laugh. "I hope you have a better poker face if you ever go to Vegas."

"It's not that I don't want to go. It's just that I have a lot of work here, and taking almost six weeks off is tough."

"Bull."

"What?"

"You know we have everything handled. And you have a cell phone and a laptop. I think there's some other reason you don't want to go."

Samantha stood up and smoothed her skirt. "Well, I don't have time to let you psychoanalyze me today, Eileen. I have to go home and pack." She shot her a fake smile as she walked across the room and opened her office door.

"Fine. But do me a favor, okay?" Eileen said as she passed her and walked into the hallway.

"What's that?"

"Try to enjoy yourself, for goodness sakes."

NOT MUCH HAD CHANGED from the last time she'd visited her sister in the sleepy little mountain town of Whiskey Ridge. Same stores, same trees, same happy looking people chatting on the sidewalks.

Meanwhile, she had already watched two condo buildings go up near where she lived in Atlanta. Progress was always happening, but Whiskey Ridge didn't know a thing about progress, apparently.

It was cute, but it was definitely stuck in some kind of time warp. On the other hand, there seemed to be no stress here. Everyone was smiling and waving and talking to each other. Where she lived, no one really talked. They all stared at their phones - herself included. She'd once watched a well dressed business woman walk right into a light pole because she was busy doing a livestream on her phone.

It was kind of funny once she was sure the woman didn't have a concussion.

Samantha drove around the square and parked for a moment. She just wanted to watch the people and drink her expensive coffee she'd picked up in the drive through outside of town. After all, what would Whiskey Ridge know about good coffee? No reason to take the chance she wouldn't be able to find something suitable.

Something about this place was appealing. She

could see why Katie moved here all those years ago. But it wasn't for her. No way. She liked the fast paced lifestyle of the big city. She liked honking car horns and the buzz that came along with packing thousands of people into a small space.

Or at least that's what she told herself.

The sudden blare of her cell phone over her car speakers scared her so much that she almost spilled her drink. She pressed the button to answer it.

"Hello?"

"Hey, sis. Where are you?" Katie asked, her upbeat voice a welcome respite from aggravated and intense clients.

"I just pulled into town."

"Always late. Hurry up!"

"I'll be there shortly," she said, rolling her eyes. Katie was free spirited, but right now she was one stressed out bride. She wasn't a bridezilla just yet, but Samantha didn't want to find out if that transformation could happen.

She pulled out of the parking space and headed toward Katie's cottage by the river. It was a beautiful place, so quaint and rustic. Samantha had only been there once, opting instead to invite Katie and Rick to her condo a few times each year.

The last time they'd come, Katie had said the

loud noises were giving her a migraine. They couldn't be any more different if they tried, she thought.

Katie was much more like their mother had been. In fact, she had spent her last summer at Katie's little house, soaking in the peacefulness of the river bubbling outside her window. That gave Samantha comfort to know her mother had been happy there, although she knew it'd been hard on Katie to have her mother pass away in the guest room.

As she pulled into the long, curved driveway, she thought about how much she was like her father. He'd been a hard charging, type A personality, winning cases left and right... but also popping acid reflux medication like the little pills were candy. Some things she wasn't happy she inherited from him.

So many days, she wished she could relax and let life happen. Even on the rare occasion she took a beach trip with her girlfriends - who she hadn't seen in months now - they'd lay on the beach getting a tan and reading books while she had to walk and dictate client notes into her phone.

Ugh. Genetics can be hard to overcome.

"Sammy!" she heard Katie yell from the front porch of the little log cabin. For as long as she'd been able to talk, Katie had called her Sammy. And for just about as long, Samantha had tried to get her to stop.

"Hey, sis!" She pulled her much shorter sister into a tight hug. They were all the family they had left, and she appreciated having time with her.

Katie was short and petite, and her fire engine red hair went with her spunky but fun personality. Samantha, on the other hand, was taller, thin and fit from her habit of running when she was stressed, and had dark brown hair like her father's had been before he went gray.

"Can you believe I'm getting married in a week?" Katie asked, a huge grin stretching across her face, pushing the freckles on her cheeks outward.

"No, I can't believe it, actually," Samantha said, flashing back in her mind to the thousands of small memories of her little sister. The princess birthday parties. The giggly "sister sleepovers" in each other's rooms. The sad days they'd had to lay their parents to rest. They'd always had each other, but life was about to change. Soon, Katie would have a husband and her own kids. Samantha felt a new kind of loneliness in the pit of her stomach.

"You okay?" Katie asked, looking concerned. Samantha immediately straightened up and smiled.

If there was one thing she'd learned as a lawyer, it was to change emotions and facial expressions on a dime.

"Of course! Help me bring my bags in, would you?"

SAMANTHA SAT at the small bistro table on her private deck overlooking the river below. The two sisters had spent the first couple of hours together getting Samantha settled in, having coffee and laughing.

But then Katie got down to business showing Samantha all of her wedding plans and giving her a tour of the house. After all, Samantha would be housesitting for a whole month, and the wedding wasn't for a couple of weeks yet. Six weeks in Whiskey Ridge was going to be a challenge.

As she stared down at the constantly moving water, she thought about how everything moved at a snail's pace here. It was so dang quiet that she could hear every thought in her head. The sound of the river was doing absolutely nothing to drown out that inner tape recorder that constantly played back all of the mistakes she'd made in her life.

"More coffee?" Katie asked from the doorway behind her.

"Nah. If I drink anymore, I'll never sleep tonight."

Katie took a seat in the chair beside her. "Oh, you'll sleep. This is the most peaceful place on Earth at night time. Crickets chirping. Owls hooting. The sound of the water flowing by."

"Sounds a little dull," Samantha said without thinking. She could see a look of hurt on her sister's face for a moment.

"You need some relaxation, Sammy."

"I disagree. Relaxation leads to thinking which leads to stress."

"Not for everyone. Maybe if you'd give this place a chance..."

"I'm here for six weeks, Katie. I think that's plenty of time, don't you?"

Katie smiled. "I could never imagine leaving here. Rick had an opportunity for a job in Chicago, helping his uncle at his shop up there. He declined."

Samantha almost swallowed her own tongue. "He declined? Chicago is an amazing city! And I bet the pay raise..."

"Stop! Jeez, Sammy. Don't you know by now that we don't want that life?"

Katie almost sounded mad, which wasn't in her

nature at all. But the frustration on her face was very evident.

"I'm sorry. I just want the best for you both."

Katie rubbed Samantha's arm. "I know you do. But what I don't understand is how you can't see that Whiskey Ridge, and this life we're building here, is what's best for us. This is our forever home. We can't wait to walk our first baby around the square in a stroller during the Fourth of July parade. And we're so looking forward to standing at the door of the elementary school and waving goodbye on the first day of kindergarten. This is where we want to build our family." She stared out at the mountains and smiled as if she was in some far away land.

"I get it. And it's a great place, sis. It really is."

"So, I have to work tomorrow, as you know. I was wondering if you could do me a huge favor?" Katie asked, a grin on her face as she pretended to pray.

"You mean aside from planning your shower, bachelorette party, being your maid of honor and housesitting for you?"

"Just one more small thing."

"What is it?"

"I need you to take Sophie to the doctor."

Sophie. Her large and very hyper two year old

boxer. The dog that bounced around like a kangaroo and passed gas like a group of bean-eating Marines.

"Katie, you know how I feel about that dog."

"I know, but she's been throwing up this week, and I just don't have time to take her during the day with my schedule. My boss is really riding me because I'll be taking so much time off after the wedding. And she's my baby!"

As if on cue, the unruly dog came bounding around the corner, sliding on the hardwood floors like she was a very uncoordinated figure skater. Unaware of how big she was, she shot straight up into Katie's lap, kissing her mercilessly.

"She looks fine now," Samantha said dryly.

Sophie jumped down and took off after the cat down the hallway. At least Whiskers had the decency to leave Samantha alone. He hid most of the time, only coming out for meals and the occasional trip to the litter box.

"She's not fine. I couldn't bear to enjoy my honeymoon if I thought Sophie could be sick…"

"Fine. I'll take her tomorrow while you're at work."

"Great! Thank you so much. I'll leave the veterinarian's business card on the counter."

"Perfect," Samantha said with a sigh. Katie leaned over and hugged her sister tightly.

"I know this is challenging for you, Sammy, but I think it's going to change your life. I really do."

She pulled back and smiled as Samantha tried to figure out what the heck that meant. But before she could ask, her sister was running back into the house.

CHAPTER 2

*S*amantha was not a morning person. She never had been, but the sound of a dog throwing up could wake even the heaviest sleeper.

As she slowly stood up from her queen sized cabin themed bed, she looked around the darkened room for the alarm clock. It was seven-thirty, and the first rays of sunlight were just starting to peek through her wooden window blinds. It took awhile for the sun to make it so far back into the darkened woods.

"I hate you, Sophie. I really do," she mumbled to herself as she pulled on the fluffy white bathrobe her sister had provided.

She opened her door and looked into the hallway. It was dark, the wood paneling not doing anything to help with the absence of light.

"Katie?" she called out. She'd forgotten to ask her sister what time she left for work, but she assumed she was home alone. The retching sound continued as she walked into the living room and found Sophie coughing up things she didn't want to see that early in the morning. "Ugh."

The dog wasn't doing well, that much was obvious. She didn't have time to even make coffee or eat breakfast - and who would have an appetite after this anyway?

After throwing on a questionable outfit of black yoga pants and ratty pink t-shirt she found in her sister's laundry pile, she loaded Sophie up into the old pickup truck Rick had given her keys to last night. There was no way she was taking the dog in her nice car, so she was thankful that she had the beat up mound of metal to cart the canine to the vet.

It wasn't that she didn't like dogs. She actually loved *well-behaved* dogs. This dog was not well-behaved. Well, she was at the moment, but only because she'd thrown up so much that she was low on energy.

Sophie laid in the seat next to her with her chin resting on her paws. She'd occasionally look up at

Samantha as she drove, but she definitely wasn't herself.

"Sorry you feel bad, girl," Samantha said. She did feel bad for Sophie. "But I have to admit that I kind of like this new laid back personality."

The dog groaned and rolled to her side.

"When I was a little girl, we had a dog named Jack. He was a Jack Russell Terrier. Kind of an obvious name. We weren't very creative people…"

Why was she talking to this dog like it understood her?

"So Jack was a little spastic, but he was smart. We trained him to do things like bring in the newspaper and turn on the TV. We were pretty lazy back in those days…"

As she drove, she looked around the small mountain town and couldn't help but smile. Everything was so simple. So easygoing. So quiet. No one was rushing. There was no real traffic. In fact, she'd only seen one traffic light in the whole town so far. And it always seemed to be green.

She pulled up in front of what was supposed to be the vet's office, but it looked more like a log cabin at the end of a gravel driveway.

"Surely this isn't a real vet's office," she said to herself. But there was a big wooden sign with the name of the place carved into it - "Ellison Veterinary Hospital". It looked like a rather new sign, but the building sure didn't look new at all. Maybe it'd been built around the time Sherman marched through Atlanta? Or when Abe Lincoln was a boy?

Samantha pulled into one of the few parking spaces in front of the place. They weren't really marked with anything except wooden logs in front of each one that were obviously there to show their width.

Before going in, Samantha called her sister just to be sure this was the right place.

"This is Katie. Can I schedule a facial for you today?" she said in her most chipper voice.

"Hey, sis. It's Samantha."

"Oh, hi, Sammy. What's up?" she asked in a whisper. Her boss apparently wasn't big on personal calls.

"Listen, I'm at what I think is your vet's office, but it looks a bit ramshackle."

"Ramshackle? Is that even a real word?"

"Google it. Anyway, are you sure you want me to take Sophie here?"

Katie giggled. "Yes, I'm sure. Dr. Ellison is a great vet."

"Okay. If you say so."

"Call me later and let me know what you find out, okay?"

Samantha hung up the phone and got out of the truck. As she walked around to the other side to open the door for Sophie, she eyed the building carefully one more time. Maybe it was supposed to have this shabby chic look. Very shabby. Not so chic.

"Come on girl," she said as she helped Sophie down from the high vehicle. The dog was able to walk, but she wasn't her normal peppy self.

Samantha pulled open the heavy door. It looked to be hand carved with an image of a bear cut into the thick wood. She coaxed the dog inside as the door slowly shut behind them.

Surprisingly, the inside wasn't as bad as she'd feared. There was a small waiting area with concrete floors, a large scale to weigh the animals and a front desk made from the same type of wood as the door.

"Can I help you, hon?" an older woman behind the counter asked. Even though she lived in Atlanta, she wasn't used to someone calling her "hon" or being so friendly. Atlanta was still a big city, after all.

"Um, yes. This is my sister's dog, and she's been sick. My sister is busy… well, she's getting married in a couple of weeks… anyway, she asked me to bring Sophie here."

The woman stared at her for a moment as if she was trying to take the information in. "Okay. What's your name, sweetie?"

"Samantha Ryan."

The woman looked down at a notepad. "Darlin', I sure don't see an appointment for you on my list."

"Right. I know. I didn't even think to call ahead. My sister just said…"

"We're real busy today, dear," she said, shaking her head. Samantha turned around and noticed only one other customer in the waiting area and at least one exam room open.

She turned back to the woman and summoned her sweetest voice. "Listen, I know I should've called. Ditzy me, I just totally forgot. It's just that this poor pup here has been throwing up something awful, and I'm worried sick about her."

The woman stared at her again, as if she was trying to figure out if Samantha was serious or was making fun of her Southern heritage and accent. She hoped it wasn't the latter because she knew first-hand that nothing was worse than ticking off a Southern woman.

"I just don't know where I'd put you…"

"Hilda? Is there a problem?" a voice said from behind Samantha. She turned and saw one of the most handsome men she'd ever seen. He had more of a tan than she'd imagined someone could get in the mountains and thick, dark hair that begged to have fingers running through it.

"Well, this lady came in without an appointment and I..."

"Oh, hey, Sophie," he said, ignoring both Hilda and Samantha as he bent down to pet the dog. "Uh oh, you definitely don't seem like yourself. Put them in room two," he said, looking back at Hilda.

Samantha watched him intently, although he didn't seem to notice her at all. Of course, today she was just wearing a pair of yoga pants and a t-shirt, but if she had her expensive business suit...

"Ma'am?" Hilda said from beside her. "Follow me."

Dr. Ellison had disappeared, so she followed Hilda - who definitely didn't seem to be her biggest fan - into the exam room.

It was small, with the same concrete floors. There was a metal table and a couple of chairs, along with the requisite pictures of dog breeds on the walls. She could hear barking from the back, but Sophie didn't seem to notice or care. She just laid down and sighed.

A few moments later, the door opened. A young woman appeared, a big smile on her face.

"Hey there, Sophie! Hi, ma'am," she said.

Why was everyone calling her ma'am? It was a little unnerving.

"Hi."

"I need to take Sophie to the back for some blood tests. Dr. Ellison will be in shortly." She took Sophie's leash and disappeared into a back room.

Samantha stared down at her phone, wondering if she should call work and check in. But she'd only been gone a day, and Eileen would probably bite her head off for not taking some time off. Unable to stop herself from thinking about work, she checked her email instead.

"Dang it!" she said out loud as she read some frustrating followup about a pending case. "Stupid idiots. They don't know who they're messing with..." she said as she typed out a response that would singe the eyelash hairs of the recipient.

"Yikes! I'd hate to be on the receiving end of that."

Dr. Ellison was standing in the doorway, and she was mortified. He slowly shut the door, smiling the whole time.

"Sorry about that. Work stuff."

"Hmm..."

"Hmm?"

"Just seems if work stuff evokes that reaction, maybe you're in the wrong business."

What was this guy's deal? Who was he to judge her?

"Excuse me?" she said, cocking her head to the side.

"No offense. I just believe you should love what you do everyday." He sat down on the rolling stool across from her, a satisfied look on his face.

"And what makes you think I don't enjoy my work? Don't you ever have a bad day as a vet?"

He thought for a moment. "Nope."

Samantha rolled her eyes. "Oh please. That's a lie, and you know it."

"You're a very blunt person, aren't you?" he said with a laugh.

"I'm not the one who came in here and judged a perfect stranger based off one small moment in time, Dr. Ellison."

"So what do you do for a living anyway?" he asked, still smiling in the most irritating - yet cute - way.

"I'm a very successful attorney in Atlanta, actual-ly," she said, sitting up straight in her chair with her chin jutted out like she was trying to win some kind of competition.

"Makes sense," he said, which just infuriated her further.

"Is this how you welcome all of your new clients?" she asked, her blood pressure starting to rise.

"First of all, they're my patients, not my clients. Secondly, Sophie has been seeing me for a few weeks now, ever since I came to Whiskey Ridge. So we're old friends."

"Well, maybe you're not a good doctor if the poor girl keeps throwing up," Samantha muttered loud enough for him to hear her. Yet again, he smiled.

"I guess your sister didn't tell you?"

Samantha furrowed her eyebrows in confusion. "Tell me what?"

"Sophie has a condition called gastroenteritis that flares up when she eats something from the yard. Being down there at the river, she gets into all kinds of stuff. We've changed her food and put her on medicine, and that keeps it at bay most of the time. But when she gets like this, Katie likes for me to check her out, do a quick x-ray, that kind of thing. We've found a few foreign objects in her stomach, all of which have passed without issue so far."

Samantha felt duped. Why hadn't her sister given her more information about Sophie's issues?

"So she's okay then?"

"Most likely. That's why my tech is running some extra bloodwork and an x-ray just to be on the safe side."

"Good. Then we'll be on our way soon," she said, looking back down at her phone.

"So what kind of law do you practice in Atlanta?"

She didn't want to make small talk with this guy, no matter how cute he was, but being trapped in a small room gave her little choice.

"Mostly corporate, but we do a variety of cases."

"Interesting."

"What about when you put a dog to sleep?"

"Excuse me?"

"You said you never have bad days as a vet. Surely, euthanizing a dog makes for a bad day?"

"Wow, you're really stuck on this, huh?"

"Just answer the question, Dr. Ellison," she said in her best cross examination voice.

"Yes, ma'am," he said, putting his hand to his forehead like a soldier.

"Don't call me ma'am. And answer the question."

"When I have to put a dog down, it's always sad, but the only time I do it is when the dog would be better off going to doggie heaven than living in pain or misery. So I don't call that a bad day because I feel like I'm doing a service to the animal and the owners. I'm able to relieve the pain, and that's a blessing."

"Oh," she said quietly.

"And we have a private pet cemetery here on the property, so my staff is able to lay our patients to rest on a rolling hillside with a small grave marker which makes our families happy because they have a place to visit."

"That's very nice," she said softly.

"So, no, I don't consider any day a bad day as a vet because I do what I love." He leaned back against the wall and smiled, obviously waiting for an answer. Or maybe an apology.

"Well, I…"

"Here's Sophie!" the perky vet tech said as she entered the room. She definitely hadn't learned the lesson of feeling the energy of a room before stepping into it.

"Hey, girl!" Dr. Ellison said, petting her head before crouching on the floor beside her. "What did the films show?"

"Nothing but a little gas," the tech said. "Still waiting for the labs to finish."

"Let me know," Dr. Ellison said before the tech left the room. He palpated the dog's belly and listened to her heart and lungs before sitting back on his stool. "Everything is looking okay. I think she got into something in the yard. I'm considering coming to Katie's house and doing some looking around in the yard just to see if I can figure out what poor Sophie here is getting into."

Coming to the house? Vets in the mountains made house calls?

"I'm sure Katie would appreciate that."

"Are you not a dog person, Miss Ryan?"

"Why would you think that?"

"It's just that you haven't been petting Sophie and you're a little standoffish to her."

She felt very uncomfortable under his gaze, like he was watching every move she made.

"As a matter of fact, I love dogs. *Well behaved* dogs, that is."

"Ah, yes. Sophie can be a bit... boisterous?" he said with a chuckle as he rubbed Sophie's head.

"I guess that's one way to put it."

"Still, if you're going to be taking care of her for awhile, you might want to build a rapport with her."

How did he know she was there for awhile?

"Labs look good," the tech said when she came back into the room.

"Okay, let's increase her meds. I'll make time to go out to the house and see if I can figure out what's making this little girl so sick," he said, rubbing her head one last time before standing up. "Your meds will be at the front desk with Hilda. Tell Katie I'll be in touch soon."

Before she could say another word, he was out of the examining room, and Samantha stood there wondering what this guy's deal was.

CHAPTER 3

Katie stood at the sink running water over the mound of lettuce. Such a simple thing, really, but Samantha couldn't recall the last time she'd done anything so domestic. She usually ordered out or had her personal chef drop by to do some batch cooking.

"So you didn't like Dr. Ellison, huh?" Katie asked with a giggle.

"He was a bit… judgmental. Critical, actually."

"What'd he say that was so critical?"

"Well, for one thing he assumed I don't like dogs."

"You don't like dogs."

Samantha was shocked that her sister would think that.

"Excuse me? I love dogs!"

"Really? When is the last time you actually had a dog?"

Samantha thought for a moment. "When we were kids."

"You mean when we had Jack?" Katie asked, her mouth hanging open.

"Yes."

"Sammy, you need a dog! You'd be so much less lonely in the big city if you had a doggie. Plus, I bet you'd meet tons of great guys at the dog park," she said as she started cutting up cucumbers.

"Oh, yes, that's what I'm aiming for. I totally want to meet a man at the dog park. Maybe we can have our first kiss while he scoops up dog excrement."

Katie rolled her eyes. "Do you ever even try to loosen up?"

"I'm as loose as I'm going to get."

Katie pulled the chicken out of the oven and peeled back the aluminum foil covering it. Samantha watched her in awe wondering how she learned all of these domestic tasks. Maybe Samantha just hadn't paid enough attention when they were growing up.

Their mother had been a fabulous cook. Apparently Samantha's apple had not only fallen far from that tree, but it had rolled down a hill and into a high-rise building with a full-time front desk staff.

"Look, I'm just saying you deserve a little happiness in your life," Katie said as she slid the chicken back into the oven.

"What makes you think I'm not happy?"

Katie stopped and put her hands on her hips. "Because I have eyes, sis. You haven't dated anyone seriously in years, and you never take any time off. I had to get married just to get you to take a vacation!"

Samantha smiled. "This isn't what I'd call a vacation."

"Well, I got you out of Atlanta and into a little peace and quiet. I've got to tell you, one of the best parts of this whole wedding and honeymoon thing is that I get to have you here. And I get to know that you're at least somewhat relaxing here in Whiskey Ridge."

"I definitely wouldn't tell Rick that having me here is the best part," Samantha said with a laugh. She'd always been uncomfortable with deep, emotional conversations.

A knock at the front door thankfully broke up their conversation. "Mind getting that?" Katie asked as she went back to work on the salad.

"Sure," Samantha said, dramatically stomping toward the front door. She pulled it open and was surprised to see Dr. Ellison standing there holding flowers. "Um, what're you doing here?"

"I was invited to dinner," he said, that irritating smile of his playing across his face.

"You brought me flowers?" she asked without thinking. Immediate regret over the assumption filled her body.

Dr. Ellison chuckled. "It's customary to bring flowers to the home owner who invited you to dinner. These are actually for Katie."

"Oh. Yeah. Right." Considering she was a top attorney, she certainly didn't have a great command of the English language right now. But there was something about this guy that just got under her skin in a way that people normally didn't.

Samantha was a tiger in the courtroom or the board room. Nobody wanted to go up against her, and everybody wanted her to represent them. She had no shortage of potential clients always waiting in line. But right now she felt like the odd man out, like she was some kind of alien living in a world she didn't understand.

"Doctor Ellison, please come in," Katie said, walking around her sister and smiling.

"These are for you," he said, his voice dripping in sarcasm as he handed the flowers to Katie.

RACHEL HANNA

"Thank you so much! Samantha, can you open the door wide enough for the good doctor here to come inside the house please?"

Samantha forced a smile and stepped back, allowing the door to open all the way. Dr. Ellison walked past her into the house to greet Rick.

"Honestly, did you have to be so rude?" Katie asked her sister in a hushed voice.

"I wasn't rude. I was just surprised to see him here."

"I invited him for dinner since he kindly offered to check out my yard to see what Sophie could be getting into."

"You could've warned me," Samantha said as she shut the door.

"Oh, I'm sorry. I didn't know I had to warn you when I invited a guest to *my* home."

Point taken, Samantha said in her own head as her sister walked away. She wasn't about to let this guy think he had her rattled. She didn't get rattled. She was the one who regularly rattled other people.

"So, Doctor Ellison, I hope you like baked chicken?" Katie said as they all stood in the kitchen.

"I love it," he said. "And please, call me Tucker."

"That just feels weird," Katie said with a laugh.

"Sometimes it feels weird to hear people call me

36

doctor," he said as he poured himself a glass of sweet tea from the pitcher on the breakfast bar. "I grew up with my father being a doctor, so I always think they're talking about him."

He smiled as he talked, and Samantha couldn't help watching him from the sidelines. Why was he so courteous and nice to Katie and not her? Well, in all fairness, maybe she wasn't the nicest to him either.

Samantha had been accused of being abrasive before, but being a woman in a male dominated industry had been tough. Rising up in the ranks had been no small feat, and she'd developed a very tough exterior that often didn't serve her well when it came to relationships.

"What kind of doctor is your father?" Katie asked as she finished chopping the last toppings for the salad.

"He was a nephrologist. Kidney doctor. But he passed away three years ago."

"I'm so sorry," Samantha heard herself say without thinking. But she knew what it was like to lose a father.

Tucker looked at her, surprised. "Thanks."

"Sammy, can you do me a favor and take Doc... Tucker, that is... out to the yard with Sophie? I'm afraid it'll be too dark after dinner, and I just need to finish a few things here."

She knew that look on her sister's face. This was some kind of set up. Something was brewing in that little head of hers.

"I think Rick knows the yard better," Samantha said through gritted teeth. Katie shot her husband-to-be a warning look.

"Um, I've actually got to make an important phone call. For work." He looked like a deer caught in the headlights. Something was definitely up.

Realizing she wasn't getting anywhere, Samantha sighed. "Fine."

She started walking out the front door with Tucker and Sophie following along behind. When they reached the porch, Sophie took off like a rocket, running all over the place.

"Is that your truck?" Sitting in front of the cabin was a large shiny red pickup truck that looked like it required a ladder to enter.

"It is," Tucker said as they walked down the steps.

"Wow. I wasn't expecting… that."

"What exactly were you expecting?"

She thought for a moment. "I don't know. Maybe a grown up type of car. Something luxurious and sleek and befitting the career you have."

"I'm a small mountain town veterinarian. I think you assume too much about my stature in the world," Tucker said with a chuckle.

"Maybe. But I get the idea that you didn't come from a place like Whiskey Ridge," she said as they walked around the side of the house.

"You're right about that. I grew up near DC, actually."

"So how in the world did you end up in this place?"

"Why do you say it like Whiskey Ridge is a step down?"

"Well, I mean… come on, Tucker. It's not exactly New York City or anything," she said with a sarcastic laugh. He stopped and looked at her like she had two heads.

"You do understand that not everyone wants to live in the big city? That some people seek out wonderful places like Whiskey Ridge because of the peacefulness and tranquility of a place like this?"

Samantha looked around. "I guess…"

He put his hand on her shoulder, which took her by surprise. "Close your eyes."

"Um, that would be a big fat no." This was how horror movies started.

"Just do it. Please. Humor me."

She sighed loudly, but closed her eyes. After a few moments, she couldn't help herself. "What am I doing exactly?"

"Shhh… Just be. Just listen."

She was quiet, but felt very silly. And then something strange started to happen. Her breathing slowed. Her mind, which raced constantly from morning until night, started to slow down too. She could hear water and birds. There were no car horns. There was a certain woodsy smell. She could hear Sophie's feet pounding the leaves as she trotted across the shady yard.

"Well?" he asked as she opened her eyes and got her bearings again.

"It's just too quiet," she said, which was actually a lie because she'd enjoyed that moment of peace. But she wasn't about to admit to it.

"I give up," he said, shaking his head. "Okay, let's get back to why we came outside. Where does Sophie normally… do her business?"

Samantha stared at him, incredulous. "Really? Do you think I have nothing better to do than follow the dog outside to watch her poop? I don't think either of us would enjoy that."

"Alright. Well, let's just watch her for a bit. Can

we sit?" He pointed to the wooden swing near the river's edge.

"Okay…"

"I'm hoping she'll forget we're here and show us what she's getting into. Jeez, are you always this suspicious?"

Samantha followed him and sat down with ample space between them. "I'm a highly paid attorney, so yes, being suspicious has given me a very nice bank account."

Tucker laughed under his breath.

"What?"

"You're very impressed with material wealth."

"Excuse me?"

"Your car. The way you dress. Talking about your success…"

"And a woman shouldn't be proud of the business she's built from nothing?"

"Of course you should be proud, but you… Never mind."

"No, please, go ahead. I can't wait to hear this," she said, rolling her eyes.

"You seem to use your intelligence and success to put up a shield."

Samantha stood up and put her hands on her hips. "Oh my gosh! Really? You have to be the most infuriating person I've ever met, Tucker. You're so critical and judgmental. You don't even know a thing about me!"

"Sit down please. I'm trying to watch Sophie, and now she's looking at you."

Samantha continued standing for a moment, but then sat down figuring Sophie would eat whatever was making her sick and this whole conversation could be over with.

"There's something about you I just don't understand," Tucker finally said.

"Oh goody. I hope you'll share your thoughts with me," Samantha said wryly.

"If you're such a successful attorney, then how is it that I'm able to rile you up so easily?"

Inside, she was seething. Partly because he was so irritating and partly because he was so right. Why did he get under her skin so badly?

"You're not riling me up. You're irritating me."

"I hope you're not like this in court. I mean, I would think it could be detrimental to your clients' cases if you freak out like this on a regular occasion."

"My clients are very happy, Doctor Ellison."

"I said to call me Tucker."

"I'd like to call you something else…"

"Oh look, Sophie's into something over there in

that area. Come on," he said, totally ignoring her comment and getting up. Against her better judgment, she followed him, mostly out of sheer curiosity as to what was making Sophie sick.

They walked to a raised vegetable patch that Katie was so proud of. It was her first garden, and she loved cooking things that came from there.

"Mystery solved," Tucker said, shaking his head and grabbing Sophie by the collar. He removed some green vines from her mouth and shooed her away. "This is what's been making Sophie sick." He held it up as if Samantha knew what it was.

"What is it?"

Tucker laughed. "You are way too much of a city girl. It's a tomato plant."

"Well, there aren't any tomatoes on it, so how was I supposed to know?"

"Any luck?" Katie asked as she walked out the back door onto the deck above them.

"This is the culprit," Tucker said, holding up the greenery. "She's been eating tomato plants. That will give a dog diarrhea and cause vomiting. You need to remove these or maybe put them in pots where she can't get to them."

"Oh wow! I had no idea that a dog would eat that!" Katie said.

"Well, Sophie's a special dog," Tucker replied with a laugh.

"Ya'll come on inside. Dinner's ready," Katie said as she called Sophie in and walked back to the kitchen.

"After you," Tucker said, pointing to the deck stairs.

"Guests should be first," Samantha said, standing her ground. Tucker just laughed again and walked up the stairs.

TUCKER COULDN'T HELP but watch her. She was an intriguing, if not snooty, woman. She was nothing like her sister. Katie was carefree, friendly and definitely a small town sort of woman. Samantha was a tough nut to crack. And thankfully, he wasn't interested in getting to know her any better than he already did.

He'd been down this road, and it was not someplace he wanted to go back to anytime soon.

But still, she was beautiful. And obviously smart. Strong willed. And surprisingly, she had girl-next-door good looks combined with chic, city style.

"And just why are you staring at me?" Samantha

suddenly asked as Tucker sat across from her at the kitchen table.

"I thought I saw a mosquito on your forehead," he said quickly. What a dumb excuse.

"So, Tucker, how are you liking it here in Whiskey Ridge," Rick asked, obviously trying to break the tension.

"I love it. The people here are very nice. Most of them, anyway."

"Was that directed at me?" Samantha asked, her voice stern like the attorney she was.

"Actually, no. Not everything is about you," Tucker said. Silence hung in the air for a moment. "I was actually talking about Nola Hughes."

"Oh goodness! Nola is known for being a pain in the backside, for sure!" Katie said with a loud laugh.

"And she has all those cats," Rick said. Tucker shot a glance at Samantha, who looked completely confused.

"Nola Hughes is the town hoarder. She hoards material possessions and animals too. Seems to take care of them pretty well, but she has sheep, dogs, cats, even a dozen or so hamsters," Katie said to her sister.

"Bet that place smells nice."

"Nobody knows since she never lets anyone on

her property. Only animal control has been there in the last few years, but she always comes out of it with her hoard of animals intact," Tucker said.

"So what brought you to this lovely little hamlet of a town?" Samantha asked, a bit of sarcasm dripping in her voice.

Tucker considered not even answering, but he didn't want to be rude to Katie and Rick. "Well, my family and I used to go camping in Whiskey Ridge when I was a kid. So when the opportunity came up to purchase old Doc Whittiford's veterinary business, I jumped at the chance."

Samantha eyed him carefully, which kind of made him uncomfortable. He bet she was a force to be reckoned with in a court room. She was definitely sizing him up, and he was afraid she'd see through his flimsy story. But if she did, she didn't say anything. She was like a shark swimming around its prey and then deciding to swim off. It wasn't like she couldn't tear him apart, bit by bit, right there at the table. It was that she chose not to.

And he was more attracted to that than he cared to admit.

CHAPTER 4

"*T*hanks for coming!" Katie yelled out the door as Tucker's large truck tossed up the red Georgia clay on Katie's dirt driveway. A plume of orange colored dust hung in the air for a few moments before Katie shut the door. "Such a nice guy, isn't he?"

Samantha rolled her eyes. "I know what you're trying to do, and it isn't going to work."

Katie walked past her into the kitchen, picking up a dish towel along the way. "And what am I trying to do?"

"You're trying to force me to like this guy so I'll move to Whiskey Ridge and live happily ever after."

Katie wiped down the countertops, brushing stray crumbs into the kitchen sink. "I'm shocked that you'd think I would stoop so low as to trick you into falling in love with an eligible, handsome doctor! Shocked, I tell you!" She held her hand to her chest in mock surprise.

"Why do you always do this?"

"Do what?"

"Try to control my life?"

"Oh come on, sis. You know that isn't true. I just want you to be happy."

"And I can't be happy in Atlanta where I live and run a very successful business?"

Katie sighed and shook her head. "See? That's what I mean."

"What?"

"It's all about money and business. When are you going to open your heart to someone again?"

Samantha stared at her hands for a moment. "The last time I did that, it didn't work out so well."

Katie dropped a coffee mug, sending it shattering all over the kitchen floor. "Dang it!"

"I'll get it," Rick said, trotting into the kitchen. "You two go relax outside on the swing. I'll finish cleaning up in here."

Katie smiled and rose up on her tiptoes to kiss him. "Thanks, sweetie. See, Sammy? You need one of these," she said, pointing to Rick.

Samantha poured another glass of sweet tea and joined her sister on the deck. Night had fallen and the sounds of the river from the blackness below was a bit spooky, but serene.

"Are you okay?" Samantha finally asked after a longer than normal silence. Katie was a talker, but she seemed nervous about something.

"I have to tell you something."

"That's never good," Samantha said as she set her tea on the glass top table next to her. She turned slightly in the swing to get a better look at her sister.

"I've put this off as long as I can, but since my shower is tomorrow…"

"What is it, Katie?"

"It's about Clark."

Samantha's breath caught in her throat. Clark? What in the world was she bringing his name up for?

"What about him?"

"He'll be at the wedding."

Samantha felt anger rise up inside of her. Clark was not someone she wanted to see again. Their failed engagement three years ago was one of the hardest times of her life. For a moment, she could see that white picket fence life in front of her, and it was snatched away when Clark suddenly said she wasn't the one for him.

Ever since, she'd buried herself in her business, which had been lucrative but soul-sucking at times. Still, there was a raw place in her heart from what Clark had said to her all those years ago.

"Why would you invite my ex fiancé to your wedding? That's just crazy!"

Katie sucked in a deep breath and blew it out. "I didn't intend for this to happen. Let me explain."

"Yes, please do." Samantha sat back and crossed her arms like a three year old, but she didn't care if it was childish. She didn't understand how her sister could do something like this to her.

"So, I take a yoga class down on the square at the spa where I work. They have a new teacher there named Monica. She's beautiful and super sweet."

"Get to the point."

"Anyway, we've become friends over the last several months. She had a boyfriend who was working overseas for some engineering firm. She talked about him all the time, and when he finally came home, he proposed to her. She was so excited and kept talking about it in class. She asked if Rick and I wanted to go on a double date…"

"Oh my gosh…"

"Right. I was so shocked when Clark comes

driving up in his sports car. My mouth dropped open. I didn't know what to do."

"So you invited them to your wedding?"

"Monica was already one of my bridesmaids, Sammy. She'd already bought her dress and had it fitted by the time I knew anything. This is very recent information…"

"And she never mentioned her boyfriend's name?"

"I guess she did, but there are other men named Clark in the world. It just never dawned on me, especially since your Clark lived in Atlanta the last time I checked."

"He's not *my* Clark," Samantha said under her breath. "I'm your sister." Now she was holding back tears, and crying wasn't something she did easily.

Katie squeezed her sister's arm. "I know, and I will un-invite them if you want me to. I just didn't know if it still bothered you…"

Samantha stood up abruptly. "Are you kidding me? Let's see… why would it bother me that the man who broke my heart three years ago is going to be at your wedding with his new fiancee? Hmmm…. Let me think…."

Katie hung her head. "I guess I thought you'd moved on, sis."

"With who?"

"Not with a person. With your life. With your business. You seem… I don't know… walled off."

"And why do you think that is?"

"Oh, come on now, Sammy. I know you loved Clark, but you weren't in love with him. You two were never compatible. Even I could see that."

"We were engaged, Katie."

"That doesn't always mean you're in love."

Samantha leaned over the railing, looking down into the darkness. "I can't believe I have to see that man again. And his perky yoga teaching fiancee. You could've warned me, Katie. Now I'm going to this wedding all alone. I'll look like an idiot in front of them."

"No, you won't, You're a strong, independent woman!"

"AKA, a sad and lonely single woman with no prospects."

Katie hugged her sister from behind, sliding her petite arms around her waist. "Now you know that's not true."

"You know I hate you, right?" Samantha asked, not meaning a word of it.

"I know. I hate me too."

Samantha tossed and turned in her bed. The quiet was enough to keep her awake at night. She was used to honking horns and the occasional siren. Now all she could hear were crickets and frogs.

This new information about Clark coming to the wedding was gnawing at her. She didn't dare to have Katie un-invite them as she didn't want to seem jealous or affected, but she was affected. Greatly, in fact.

She'd met Clark in Atlanta when he was a witness at a civil trial she was involved in. It was just a business case, but his engineering expertise had been a godsend, and it helped her client win a multi-million dollar lawsuit.

Love hadn't bloomed immediately, but over the few weeks they'd worked together, she found it to be comfortable spending time with him. He wasn't as fast paced as she was, and he donated his time to charitable causes when she was too busy to see him. Samantha didn't have much free time as she was building her client base and trying to keep her eye on the prize.

Still, they eventually started dating seriously, and

Samantha had started to see a life with Clark. They traveled together when she could get time off, and they spent lazy Sundays drinking coffee in her apartment and reading the newspaper. It felt like there might be a future, and when Clark proposed over dessert at a fancy restaurant one night, she felt a different kind of hope for her future. Maybe a house. Maybe kids.

But three months after their engagement, Clark abruptly called it off. He said they weren't compatible and that she was too caught up in her work. He said she didn't have enough time for him, and he didn't think that would ever get better. He wanted something else.

Samantha had given back her beautiful ring, changed her social media relationship status back to single and sulked in her apartment with tubs of ice cream for days. But, in true Samantha fashion, she'd eventually used her personal pain to win cases for her clients. And her business flourished because of it.

Never again had she planned to see Clark. And now she'd see him within days. And she'd see his fiancee tomorrow. This was turning out to be a very long visit to Whiskey Ridge, and it was only the second day.

"Isn't this place beautiful?" Katie asked excitedly as they stood in the rented ballroom space.

"Yes, it is," Samantha said, nervously looking around for any sign of Clark or his fiancee.

"The shower will be in that room over there, and we'll hold the reception in this big ballroom after we get married at the church next door," she repeated for the third time since they'd gotten there. Katie was definitely anxious about her wedding day.

"I think I see some cars pulling in," Samantha said as she peered out the window.

"Yay! I can't wait. I love presents!" Katie was still such a kid at heart, and Samantha envied that about her. She was always so positive and happy, no matter the circumstance.

A few minutes later, women started pouring into the building, each one hugging Katie as they made their way to the room where the shower was being held. Samantha, realizing she was the official hostess, did her best to smile and shake hands with each and every stranger. All the while, she kept an eye out for a hot woman in yoga pants, but no such woman appeared.

"I'd like to welcome you all to my baby sister's

bridal shower," Samantha said as she stood at the front of the room. She was no stranger to speaking in public, so at least this part should be a breeze, she thought to herself. "Katie, I know Mom would be so proud of the woman you've become and the choice you've made in a husband. I wish you and Rick all the happiness in the world…"

Before she could finish her thought, a young woman snuck into the room, hugging people along the way. She was firm and curvy at the same time, with her long auburn hair and bright blue eyes. It had to be Monica.

"Sammy, are you okay?" Katie asked in a loud whisper as she waited for her sister to finish her sentence. She was suddenly aware of everyone staring at her.

"Yes, sorry. Lost my train of thought there for a second. So, let's all raise our punch cups to Katie and wish her well in her new journey as a wife!"

As everyone cheered and clinked their little plastic wine glasses together - which made a very odd sound - Samantha slinked to the side of the room and sat down. Katie soon followed.

"What happened up there?"

"That's her, isn't it?"

Katie craned her head and looked through the

group of people before hanging her head and turning back to Samantha.

"Yes."

"My God, she's like a freaking model," Samantha said. "And Clark isn't even that good looking. I mean he's okay, but…"

"Apparently he really romanced her," Katie said.

"Well, if she was the prize, then I guess so. Men can be so…"

"Katie!" Monica said as she ran over to her. Katie stood as Monica hugged her tightly. "You look adorable! Where did you get that cute little dress?"

Katie shot a glance down at her sister. "I got it at Callie's Dress Shop over on Elm. Have you been there?"

"Not yet, but I'm definitely going to! Your shower is just beautiful. I love all the decorations."

"Thank you. Actually, my sister here did all of this," Katie said, pointing down at Samantha.

"Your sister? Oh, wow. This is a little awkward," she said with a smile and a slight look of what appeared to be pity. "Hi. I'm Monica," she said, reaching out her perfectly manicured hand to Samantha.

"Hi," Samantha said, quickly shaking her hand before standing up. "Oh, dang. I totally forgot to bring out the cupcakes. They have little wedding dresses on them. Just adorable! I must go grab them from the fridge. Super excited to meet you!" she said in her fakest voice with an even faker smile, before making a quick escape to the back room.

She closed the door behind her, needing a moment alone to catch her breath. Why was this all so upsetting to her? That might require some soul searching, and she hated soul searching.

But soon she heard a click alerting her that the door was opening. Why couldn't she just get a moment of peace?

"Katie, I…"

"It's not Katie."

Clark. His booming voice was unmistakable. She wanted to throw up.

Samantha slowly turned around and saw him standing there across the room. It'd been three years since she'd seen him last, but he looked much the same. Preppy clothing, short haircut, no facial hair. He looked like he stepped right off the golf course in his khaki shorts and pale pink polo shirt.

"Hi, Clark."

"Hey, Sam. It's really good to see you."

"Is it?"

"Of course. It's been so long," he said as he

crossed the room with his big toothy smile. Without warning, he hugged her. She didn't reciprocate, and he quickly pulled back.

"Why are you at a bridal shower?"

"I'm actually not. I just brought..." He stopped short of finishing his sentence.

"Don't worry. I already know about Monica."

He let out a relieved breath. "Good."

"She's very pretty," Samantha said as she leaned against the wall.

"That she is. But she's so much more than that, Sam. She's smart and talented and loving."

"Ah, so the exact opposite of me?"

Clark rolled his eyes. "Really? This is how you're going to act? Defensive and sarcastic? I see not much has changed." He turned to walk toward the door.

"Actually, a lot has changed," Samantha said loudly.

Clark turned back to her. "Oh yeah? And what is that?"

And then she said it - the dumbest thing she'd said in a long time. Maybe ever.

"I'm engaged too."

SAMANTHA SAT in her chair beside Katie and watched her open her gifts. She plastered a big smile on her face as she wrote down what was in each package and the person who gave it so that Katie could send thank you notes later.

She was really trying to enjoy the moment, but all she could think about was the big, fat lie she'd just told to Clark before basically sprinting out of the room with the excuse that she needed to be there for her sister.

But the look on Clark's face had said it all. He was stunned, maybe even more than she was at her own stupidity. Now she'd painted herself into a very tiny corner that there was no way out of. And when her sister found out, she was going to laugh and point her finger. This was a huge mess.

Right now, her best bet was to keep Clark and Monica away from Katie until she could tell her what she'd done. And then she would make up another huge lie about how her fiancé was on a secret mission somewhere and unable to attend the ceremony. Yeah, they would definitely believe that.

"Look, Sammy! Isn't this beautiful?" Katie said, holding up an ivory silk and lace peignoir set that Monica had given to her.

"Gorgeous," Samantha said, smiling so hard that

her jaw was starting to lock. She really did want to be the bigger person, but instead she felt like she was reverting back to middle school. Or maybe they were more mature than she was. Whiskey Ridge had to be affecting her. Perhaps the air was too thin in the mountains?

Katie finished opening her gifts and guests finally started to leave. But not Monica. Nope, she was apparently hanging around until the very last second.

"Sammy, this was an amazing shower. Thank you," Katie said, hugging her.

"You're welcome," Samantha said louder than needed. "I told Clark I'm engaged so don't be surprised if he says something to you," she whispered into her sister's ear.

Katie pulled back, her eyebrows knitted together. "What?"

"Beautiful shower, Katie Poo!" Monica said, running up and hugging her.

"Katie Poo?" Samantha muttered under her breath. Monica shot her a look, but didn't say anything.

"I have to get going, but I'll see you at your bachelorette party tomorrow night!" The two women squealed like schoolgirls before Monica trotted off like some kind of high school cheerleader, yoga-teacher robot with the perfect butt.

Samantha finally let out the breath she'd been holding for the last hour. Katie waved at the last few guests before turning back to her sister.

"What in holy heck is going on?" she asked, throwing her hands up in the air.

"I know, I know. I'm so sorry. I didn't mean to ruin your shower…"

"Sammy, you didn't ruin my shower. It was lovely," she said, putting her hands on Samantha's shoulders. "But I am wondering what's going on in that very intelligent mind of yours?"

"I don't know! Whiskey Ridge is making me some kind of stupid, immature middle schooler."

"Yeah, I don't think Whiskey Ridge is doing that."

"I feel like I'm losing my mind here, and it's only been a couple of days," Samantha said, hanging her head. "I'm never like this, sis. You know that."

"You have been a little… scattered… since you got here."

Samantha stood up and walked over to her sister's table full of gifts. She ran her fingers across one of the frilly bows.

"You know, I really thought Clark and I were going to make a go of it at the time. I kept picturing the big house in the suburbs that we'd buy and the huge swing set he'd build on his days off. We'd have two kids, a boy and girl, of course."

Katie slid her arms around her sister. "I'm so sorry, Sammy. I had no idea you were so domestic."

Samantha turned and straightened. "I'm not. It was temporary insanity."

Katie stepped back and sighed. "It's okay to want a family."

"Look, this day… actually, this whole month… is about you and Rick. I'm sorry I made it about me. It won't happen again, okay? Let's just forget this ever happened and enjoy this wonderful time in your life. You're going to be such a beautiful bride."

Katie smiled. "Changing the subject. Such an old tactic."

"And yet such a good one, right? Come on, you promised to take me by to see your dress."

CHAPTER 5

*S*amantha looked at her tablet carefully. "Okay, the Bremont case should be wrapping up by the end of the week. Tell Hal that we aren't budging on those revisions we made to the contract."

"Yes, Boss," Eileen said from the other end of the phone line. Managing her booming business from two hours away was proving to be challenging. Samantha definitely liked having more control over the day to day running of her business.

"And then I need you to check on the status of the Moore contract. If we can't come to terms on that, we'll have to take it to court. I really don't want to do that because Abe Moore is a very unpleasant man to deal with. And he smells weird. I hate being cooped up in a conference room with that man."

"Got it. Order air fresheners for the conference room..."

"Don't forget next Thursday, I need someone to file the merger papers on the Lyle case."

"Right."

"Any questions?"

"Yes. Can we go back to the beginning of this conversation where you accidentally blurted out that you're pretend engaged to an invisible mountain man?" Eileen asked. Silence hung in the air.

"I'm just a little tired."

"And being tired made you invent a fiancé?"

"Not funny."

Eileen giggled. "I don't think I've ever heard you as rattled as you seem to be now. Are you okay?"

"I'm telling you, it's the air up here."

"Doubtful."

"It's just that seeing Clark and his perfect little yoga teacher fiancee made me feel..."

"Jealous?"

"No!"

"Envious?"

"Isn't that basically the same thing?"

"Nauseous?"

"That's more like it."

"Look, I was there for the whole Clark fiasco. I know how much you were planning on a life with him. But come on, Sam, you know you two were never right for each other. He wanted something... else."

"Thanks for reminding me how unwanted I was."

"That's not what I meant, and you know it. Clark wanted a woman who would dote on him. He wanted someone he could control, and that definitely isn't you."

"Just forget it, okay? I'm tired of talking about it, and tonight is my sister's bachelorette party. I need to get myself together and focus on making this event about her and not myself. From now on, I'm going to be the perfect maid of honor."

"Well, if you're an expert at anything, it's perfection," Eileen said dryly. "Gotta go. The pizza and male escorts just arrived."

"Very funny," Samantha said, but Eileen had already ended the call. She sat for a moment wondering if she was serious about those escorts. And then she wondered how much it would cost to hire a really hot looking one and make him drive to Whiskey Ridge.

THE NIGHTCLUB they'd chosen for Katie's final night as a single woman was just outside of Whiskey Ridge in a little shadier part of town. It was like something straight out of a Western movie, complete with rough looking wood floors and a real jukebox blaring 90s country music.

But Katie was having the time of her life, and that was all that mattered.

"Woo!" Katie howled as she danced on one of the big wooden boxes strewn around the edges of the dance floor. She might've had one too many glasses of wine. Katie never drank. She was way too petite and a lightweight. But here she was, dancing away with the biggest grin on her face.

Samantha watched her sister from the red fake leather bar stool where she'd perched as soon as the other bridesmaids had climbed up to dance too. She felt like a stick in the mud, but she just wasn't the type to climb up on furniture to "shake her groove thang".

"Not enjoying the party?" she heard someone say from the stool beside her. She turned around and was shocked to see Tucker sitting there with a smile on his face. Man, he was looking extra hot this evening with his plaid shirt and distressed jeans. And were those actual cowboy boots?

"What are you doing here?"

"Believe it or not, this is one of my favorite places to come on a Friday night. Am I to assume this is the bachelorette party Katie was talking about?"

"This is it," Samantha said, taking a drink of her water. She wasn't much of a drinker. It took the control away, and she definitely didn't like that feeling.

"Looks… raucous," he said with a laugh.

She smiled. "They're a little tipsy on wine and love, I think."

"And you're drinking…"

"Water. On the rocks. With lemon."

Tucker chuckled. "Designated driver?"

"That and I really don't drink much. Not my thing."

He eyed her for a moment. "What *is* your thing, Samantha?"

"Don't start an argument."

"I'm not trying to. I really want to know what you like. What gets your motor running?"

She rolled her eyes. "Okay, fine. I don't have anything better to do so I'll play along. I like research. I like to argue in court. I like to win."

"I mean aside from work. What makes you happy? I think I already know it doesn't involve dogs."

She sighed. "Again, I told you I actually like dogs."

"Right. Anyway, what are your hobbies?"

"I don't have hobbies. Those are what I call time wasters."

"Wow." He shook his head and took a long draw of his beer.

"Wow?"

"It's sad." He actually did look stunned. And a little sad.

"Why is that sad? I love my career."

"There's more to life than work, Sam," he said. That was the first time he'd shortened her name. She liked it more than she cared to admit.

"Maybe so, but right now work comes first."

"And when do you come first?"

"I don't understand?"

He turned slightly in his seat. "I've learned that if you don't do things that bring you joy, you'll never be truly happy." He was so serious that she almost didn't breathe for a moment.

"So what brings you joy?"

He turned back toward the bar and smiled. "Animals, of course. But I also like kayaking. Fishing. Hiking."

"Ah, you're an outdoorsy guy."

"Somewhat. But I also love art museums, classical music and… don't tell anyone this… cooking."

"Cooking? Really? What do you cook really well?"

He thought for a moment. "I make an amazing pineapple chicken with this rosemary balsamic sauce on the side."

"That sounds great right about now. All we've had tonight were what I think were chicken fingers and very greasy french fries," she said, looking back at her sister who was still dancing up a storm. "But look at her. She's so happy."

Tucker watched her for a moment. "And you just smiled."

Samantha turned back to him. "You didn't know I could smile?"

"I've never seen it, but it looks nice. You should find more things that make you do that."

Suddenly, she felt the strange sensation of butter-flies in her stomach. Why was he affecting her this way? She didn't want to like him, but there was something about their banter that made her want to stay and talk to him all night.

"So, the wedding is tomorrow night, huh?" he finally said after an awkward silence on her end.

"Yes. It's going to be lovely. Katie and Rick deserve a big, beautiful wedding and a great life together."

"What about you?" he asked. Man, this guy had a lot of questions.

"What about me?"

"You never wanted that married, domesticated lifestyle?"

She hesitated for a moment. "Nope. Not me."

"You're lying."

"Now, see? You were being so nice for a second. A literal second." She turned back to her water and took a long swig, hoping he'd change the subject. No such luck.

"Come on, we're forging this new friendship so tell me your deepest, darkest secrets and dreams," he said with a laugh.

"Fine. Yes, at one time I did want the whole white picket fence thing. But that changed."

"Why'd it change?"

"Well…" she started to say, but then she turned to see Monica grinning from ear to ear and running across the dance floor. And then there he was again. Clark. "Ugh."

Tucker turned slightly and seemed to notice the commotion. "Who's that?"

"My ex-fiance and his new bride to be," she said, putting her finger down her throat and gagging.

"And the plot thickens…"

"Long story short, he dumped me because I wasn't good enough for him, apparently. That was three years ago. Had no idea he was here or that his girlfriend was one of the bridesmaids. And then I panicked at the shower and lied about having a fiancé of my own. I'm an idiot," she said, putting her head in her hands.

"Wait, what?"

"Hey, Sam." How Clark had made it across the club in such a short time period was a mystery to her. But there he stood, a smug look on his face with Monica hanging on his arm. She was obviously tipsy.

"Clark. Barbie."

"You know her name is Monica."

"Sorry. Seems like maybe she needs a ride home," Samantha said as she watched Monica slide into a nearby chair and lay her head on the table.

"Yeah, she's had a little too much fun tonight. So, who's this?" he asked, pointing at Tucker.

"Dr. Tucker Ellison. And you are?" Tucker said

with an authority she hadn't seen before. He stood up and towered above Clark's skinny frame, sticking out his hand.

"Clark. Are you, uh, Samantha's fiancé?"

Time stood still as Samantha opened her mouth to say no. Instead, Tucker's voice overshadowed her own.

"Yes, I am."

What? Samantha's eyes popped open as she struggled to get air. Instead, she choked and had to grab her glass of water.

"Samantha didn't tell me she was dating a doctor," Clark said, a hint of sarcasm in his voice.

"Well, she didn't tell me a darn thing about you at all," Tucker said with a wry smile. "Were you her tax accountant or something?"

Clark straightened. "I was her fiancé. Three years ago, anyway."

Tucker slid closer to Samantha and put his arm around her, causing her face to push into his lower chest as he stood. "Sorry you let a beautiful woman like this go, but I guess that's just my good fortune, huh?"

Clark looked dumbfounded, his mouth almost hanging open. With no other options, he woke Monica up and ushered her to the door, quickly saying "goodbye" and "nice to meet you" as he almost sprinted out of the place.

When he was gone, Samantha faced Tucker.

"Have you lost your ever loving mind?"

Tucker smiled like he was proud of himself. "I was in high school theater. I think my performance was top notch."

"Now what are we going to do?"

"Well, it looks like I now have a date for your sister's wedding?"

"I really don't like you right now, Tucker."

He smiled down and tilted her chin up. "See you tomorrow night."

KATIE STIRRED IN THE BED, a groan escaping her lips as her sister leaned over and pressed a cold cloth to her forehead.

"What time is it?" she whispered, her voice sounding two octaves lower than normal.

"It's six in the morning," Samantha responded.

"Oh no! It's my wedding day, and I feel terrible!"

Samantha rubbed her sister's arm. "Don't worry. I'm going to pump you full of water and aspirin, and you'll be good as new by tonight."

"I can't believe I drank that much wine. What was I thinking?" she asked as she slid upright onto her pillow and leaned her head back. Samantha sat next to her, their heads atop each other.

"I believe you said 'woo hoo', so I'm assuming that's what you were thinking most of the time."

Katie laughed and then groaned again. "It was a very memorable evening. I think. I can't really remember a lot of it. Was I dancing on a box?"

"Quite a bit, yes."

She put her hand over her eyes. "I'm so embarrassed."

"Don't be. It was your last night of freedom, and you made the most of it."

Katie looked up at her sister. "Well, you look fine so how did you manage that?"

"I steered clear of wine bottles and big wooden boxes."

"Designated driver. I remember now."

"Plus you know I'm not a big drinker anyway."

"So what did you do with all those hours? Just sit and watch us be idiots?"

Samantha swallowed hard. "Sort of."

Katie looked at her and raised an eyebrow. "What aren't you telling me?"

"Well... Long story short... Clark showed up to

pick up his very tipsy fiancee, and Tucker was there too…"

"Tucker? Why was he there?"

"Don't know, but he landed smack dab next to me at the bar."

"And?"

"When Clark started prodding me about my fiancé, Tucker suddenly stood up and said he was my fiancé."

"What?" Katie said, sitting up so fast that she had to grab her head to stop it from swimming. "Why would he do that?"

Samantha smiled slightly. "Honestly, I still don't know. All I know is he said he was my date for the wedding and he'd see me tonight."

Katie grinned like a Cheshire cat. "Ooohhh… I think he likes you…"

Samantha stood up and walked across the room for a bottle of water. "Um, no. He can't stand me. And I feel similarly."

"Right. So why would he save you like that?"

"Who said he saved me?"

"Come on, Sammy. You know that you wanted to save face with Clark, and Tucker rode in on a white horse and helped you do just that."

Samantha handed the water to her sister. "Drink.

We've got to flush your system out." Katie obliged and took a long sip. "Either way, I need to go talk to Tucker today and explain that I don't need his help."

"Are you kidding me?"

"No. Why?"

"This is perfect. Just let Clark think that you're engaged to a handsome doctor. That way you can enjoy the wedding without worrying about him finding out about your big fat lie."

"You're funny. Do you honestly think I can spend a whole evening with Tucker Ellison? I mean, without trying to strangle him with your veil?"

Katie smiled. "Come on, sis. It's one night. You might actually have fun."

"Doubtful. He's arrogant and critical and…"

"I get it. You're not a fan. But this will all be over soon, and you can go back to Atlanta with your pride in tact."

"And what happens a few months from now when Clark asks about my future husband and our wedding plans?"

"What do you care? You'll be back home enjoying the fancy life, right?"

Samantha thought for a moment. "I guess so. But still, I need to go see Tucker and make sure he wasn't a little tipsy too when he agreed to this whole thing."

∾

TUCKER PEERED into the German Shepherd's ear. "It's definitely irritated. Looks like an allergy of some kind. I recommend diphenhydramine for a few days, and I'll give you some cream you can rub into it every night to get it to heal."

"Thank you, Doctor Ellison. Poor Mavis has been scratching her brains out for days now," the older woman said.

"Just follow Amy up front, and she'll get you all squared away," he said, smiling as he gave the dog another quick scratch on her head. She followed his vet tech to the front desk as he slipped into the back room. This was the only place to really get away for a few minutes in his busy veterinary practice. He loved his work more than anything, but it did get lonely at times.

Since his divorce two years ago, Tucker had been more walled off than he'd ever been in his life. The breakup of his marriage was something he'd never expected, and sometimes he felt like he should never let anyone else into his heart again.

His ex wife, Susan, had been his perfect match when they'd met in college. He thought they'd spend their lives raising a family together, but when she'd changed her mind about having kids a few months into their marriage, he'd been devastated.

Tucker wanted a family. He wanted at least a couple of kids, and he wanted a stable home life. But Susan had decided she wanted to be child-free. Not only that, but she wanted to travel full-time and blog about it. While he wanted to support her dreams too, he couldn't run his veterinary practice on the road.

Before long, their marriage was in shambles because they wanted such different things. And then Susan had decided she wanted another man. And then she was gone, globe trotting around the world with a guy she'd met in a local cooking class. She'd even requested the final divorce papers be sent to her current location in Vietnam where she was backpacking in some remote area and tasting the local cuisine.

Sometimes, in his lonelier moments, or when he was sticking a thermometer in the hind end of an unhappy canine, he wondered if he'd made the right decision. What if she had been the love of his life? The one he was meant to be with until he took his last breath?

He didn't like to think about it, but sometimes his brain overtook him.

His parents had been married over forty years when his father passed away, and he wanted a love like that. He wanted a forever partner who would stand by him no matter what. So there were moments he wondered if he should have supported Susan's free spirit and gone along for the ride.

Still, every time he saved a dog's life or scratched a cat's belly, he knew he was working in his calling. It was all so confusing.

Right now, he was wondering what on Earth made him stand up and pretend to be Samantha Ryan's fiancé last night. It seemed like he was dreaming, or maybe having a nightmare.

There really hadn't been a valid reason why he'd done it. Something inside of him just felt protective of her in that moment, although he'd never tell her that. She'd probably sock him between the eyes if she knew that he was trying to protect her.

Now, he had a date to a wedding with a woman who couldn't stand him. And he had to pretend he loved her. What had he gotten himself into?

"Excuse me, Doctor Ellison, but there's a woman here to see you."

CHAPTER 6

Samantha sat in the wooden rocking chair, watching the animals come in and out of Tucker's practice. He seemed pretty successful, from the looks of it.

"Ma'am? You can follow me," the young woman said as she led Samantha through a swinging wooden door. "He's right in there."

She walked through another doorway and saw Tucker sitting in a plush arm chair, drinking a glass of sweet tea.

"Working hard I see," she said wryly.

"Even I take a break now and then," he replied, setting his drink on the side table and smiling. "What can I do for you?"

Samantha smirked. "Really? Don't you remember the mess you got me in last night?"

"Mess? As I recall, you lied to your ex and told him you were engaged. I had no part of that."

Samantha sat down in the chair across from him. "True, but you didn't have to identify yourself as my future husband."

Tucker leaned back. "No, I didn't, but I thought I was helping you."

"Why would you want to help me anyway? You hate me, Tucker."

He furrowed his eyebrows. "I don't hate anyone, Samantha. Even my ex wife." Right after he said it, he seemed to regret it.

"You have an ex wife? This is new information."

"Let's not go there. Why are you here?" His voice was firmer than she'd heard it before, so she decided not to push.

"I'm giving you the option to back out."

He looked surprised. "You're afraid to go with me?" That smirk was both sexy and slap-inducing.

"I'm not afraid of anything, Doctor Ellison," she said, in her best attorney voice. "I just wanted to give you an out."

"I didn't ask for an out."

They seemed to be at an impasse.

"Well, then, I hope you're a great actor," she said as she stood up.

Tucker stood and closed the space between them. "I'm a fantastic thespian," he said softly. Samantha felt a shiver she didn't expect.

"Oh yeah?" was all she could muster, her heartbeat quickening.

"High school theater club president."

"Nerd?" she said shakily.

Tucker smiled and stepped back a few inches. "I hope you can do this."

"Why would you think I couldn't?"

"Because I just got close to you, and you looked like you wanted to crawl out of your skin."

"You have a way with women," she said sarcastically. She wasn't about to admit that the closer he got, the more she wanted to take a good nibble at his neck.

"Sam, if this is going to work, you have to make Clark believe you're so in love with me that you are going to be my wife. Can you do that?"

Just the mention of Clark made her tense up. She wanted to make him think she'd moved on and that he hadn't gotten the best of her. Anything was better than that.

"I can do it. Can you?"

"I told you. I'm a great actor," he said, shrugging his shoulders and smiling.

"Great."

"I'll pick you up at six?"

"Five. I have to be at the church early. I am the maid of honor, remember," she said with a slight smile as she turned for the door.

"Right. I'll see you then."

Samantha turned back around. "Oh, and make sure to look good. I wouldn't get engaged to a slob," she said with a wink.

"I'M SO NERVOUS!" Katie said as she sat at her small white vanity. She'd chosen to get ready at home, but she would put her wedding dress on in the bridal room at the church.

"Don't be! You're marrying your Prince Charming," Samantha said as she put her arms around her sister from behind and looked in the mirror. "Mom would be so proud of you, Katie."

Katie's eyes welled with tears. "I miss her so much, especially today. And Daddy. I wish…"

"I know."

"But you're here," she said, pulling her sister's arms tighter around her. "And it means the world."

"Of course. I wouldn't be anywhere else. You know that," Samantha said. "Now, dry those eyes because I'm not sure your mascara is waterproof."

Katie went back to working on her makeup. "Listen out for the door because the girls should be here soon."

Samantha nodded and walked to the kitchen for a drink of water. She knew what "the girls" meant. Katie had three bridesmaids in addition to her, and one was Monica. She wasn't ready to spend the afternoon with that woman.

"Knock knock!" she heard as Monica let herself in, trailed by the other two very nice woman whose names Samantha couldn't remember to save her life. "Oh. Samantha. Hello." It was clear that Monica didn't like her either.

"Howdy," Samantha said, for reasons she couldn't understand.

"I assume Katie's back there?"

"Yep."

Monica looked at her for a moment and then walked down the hallway. Much to her chagrin, Samantha was forced to follow her since she was the maid of honor and couldn't just run screaming into the forest behind the house.

"Aw, you look simply stunning!" Monica said, her own makeup rivaling that of a drag queen, Samantha thought to herself. A giggle escaped her lips.

"Sammy, do I not look good?" Katie asked, peering around Monica's waist.

"Oh, of course you look beautiful! I was just thinking about something else. I wasn't laughing at you."

Katie watched her for a few seconds longer before leaning back.

"Maybe let's add just a touch of highlights right here," Monica said, itching to take over Katie's makeup process.

"Oooh, yes, that looks wonderful!" one of the other women said. They all giggled and cooed like teenagers in front of the mirror, and Samantha had to admit she was feeling a bit left out. She'd never fit in with other girls, sometimes even her own sister. Although she liked fashion - the expensive kind - she wasn't someone who was into makeup or hair. She only got hers done because she needed to look a certain way in her line of work. At home, she was more a yoga pants and t-shirt kind of woman.

But this was her sister's big day, and she was going to start her acting debut right now if it killed her. So she joined in the oohing and ahhhing and smiled her biggest toothy grin until it was time to go to the church.

As Tucker drove down the dirt driveway, he thought about the night ahead of him. How was he supposed to pretend to be in love with a woman who seemed to dislike him with every fiber of her being? High school thespian or not, he wasn't sure why he was doing this. He could easily turn around, go back home and watch mindless westerns on TV. But he wouldn't because that wasn't the kind of man he was.

He was loyal, always to a fault, and not always to the right people. Even if she was almost a stranger to him, he'd made a commitment, and he was going to keep it. But as soon as he pulled up and saw Clark getting out of his car, he felt like turning around again. He didn't like that guy. Not one bit.

"Hey," Clark said as he straightened his black tux and locked his door with the remote.

"Hey." Tucker climbed out of his truck and reached for his tuxedo jacket hanging on a hook in the rear seat.

"Here to pick up Sam, I guess?"

Tucker put on his jacket and looked at Clark. "Of course. I wouldn't let my fiancee hitch a ride to the service, would I?"

The two men walked toward the door. "So how long have you two been together?" Clark asked, his curiosity getting the better of him apparently.

"Long enough," Tucker said before knocking on the door.

The tension between them was palpable, and honestly he didn't know why he disliked Clark so much. Maybe it was his scrawny body shape or his weasel-like little eyes or his high pitched, irritating voice that didn't seem to make it all the way through puberty. Or maybe Tucker was imagining that he was quite that bad.

"Hey, sweetie," Monica said as she opened the door and basically fell into Clark's arms. The whole thing was a bit much, in Tucker's opinion. It was like they were putting on a show.

But he himself was about to put on a show as well.

And when he saw Samantha approaching the foyer, his heart literally skipped a beat. Wearing a pale pink gown that revealed one shoulder, she looked beautiful. And this whole thing suddenly felt a lot harder.

"Wow. You look stunning, Sam," he said to his own amazement. Right now, she wasn't the woman he'd been sparring with for days. She was a gorgeous maid of honor, and his pretend fiancee.

She almost seemed to blush a bit and smiled. Tucker was very aware at the strange way Clark and Monica were actually watching them, as if they were wondering when one of them would slip up.

Tucker leaned in and kissed Sam on the cheek quickly. "Guess we'd better go?"

"Yes. Katie is riding with one of the other brides-maids, so we'll just meet her there."

Tucker took her hand and helped her down the wooden stairs toward the truck.

"Do you think they bought it?" she whispered under her breath.

"I don't know. But we definitely have a long night ahead of us."

KATIE STOOD in front of the mirror and smoothed out her dress. It was just her and Samantha for a few moments.

"I saw him kiss you," she said quietly.

"On the cheek. No big deal."

"Oh please. You're enjoying this," Katie said with a giggle.

"No, I most definitely am not enjoying this."

"Pretty soon, maybe you'll be standing here in a white gown of your own."

"Only if they admit me to the mental hospital after this whole fiasco is over."

Katie sighed. "I hope you at least try to enjoy the wedding."

"Oh, sis, I'm looking forward to watching you and Rick take your vows. I don't want this to be about me and my stupid lie. If you want, I'll walk out there and tell Clark the truth right now. In fact, that's what I'm going to…"

"No. You're not doing that!" Katie said, grabbing her arm.

"Why? It's going to come out anyway at some point when I don't actually get married. Better to rip the bandage off now."

Katie touched her sister's cheek. "I want to see

my sister have a fantastic night with a handsome man, even if he is her pretend fiancé. Okay?"

"I shouldn't care what Clark and Monica think."

"But you do. You're human, Samantha Ryan, even if you don't want the world to believe it. Just have fun tonight. Let loose. Be open to possibilities."

Samantha rolled her eyes. "You're really a hopeless romantic, aren't you?"

"Hey, I didn't get into this wedding dress without being a hopeless romantic," she said with a laugh.

"Katie? We're almost ready for the ceremony to start." The wedding planner, Elouise, poked her head into the bridal room. She was almost as old as the hills and as round as the bales of hay in the field behind the church, but she was a dang good wedding planner that kept things moving right along.

"Ooohhh this is it," Katie said to her sister, rubbing her hands together. "I can't wait to be Rick's wife!"

The look of excitement on her face was something Samantha longed for. She wanted a man to come home to after a long day. She wanted a soft place to fall. She wanted someone who would wrap her up in his arms and shield her from the world. And she didn't want anyone to know that because to be that vulnerable felt dangerous to her.

"Ready?" Samantha asked. Katie nodded quickly, a huge grin on her face.

"Let's do this!"

THE WEDDING HAD BEEN beautiful and had gone off without a hitch. Samantha was thrilled for her sister, but her anxiety was growing the more she thought about the reception. How was she going to spend all that time with Tucker without Clark catching on to her ruse?

"Hey there," Tucker said when he found her outside of the church. She was busy taking pictures with the rest of the bridal party and some of Rick's family.

"Hey. Sorry for the wait. We should be done here in a few minutes."

"No problem. I'll meet you by the tree over there."

Samantha nodded and couldn't help but smile. He really wasn't all that bad tonight. In fact, he was kind of nice.

"I see your fiancé is waiting for you over there," Katie whispered as she joined Samantha while she waited for Rick's side of the family to get some photos.

"Funny."

"He really looks handsome tonight."

"Don't you already have a husband?" Sam said with a chuckle.

"I won't rest until my wonderful sister has one too," Katie said grinning and then trotted away.

Samantha had a feeling she was being very serious.

WHEN PICTURES WERE DONE, it was time to join the rest of the guests at the reception in the ballroom next door. Samantha made her way to find Tucker at the tree, and he was still there leaning against the rough bark, staring at the church with a far away look in his eyes.

"What are you looking at?"

"Oh nothing. I just love old churches like this. So much history, ya know?" he said as they started to walk.

"Yeah, it's nice."

"Don't you ever look at something like that and think about all of the church services and weddings and funerals that have been held in a building like that?"

"Not really," she said with a laugh.

"All of the tears that have been cried, both joyful ones and sorrowful ones…"

"You're an emotional guy, aren't you?"

"Not really. But I'm not afraid of it either."

"Was that a dig? Already?" she asked, looking at him.

Tucker stopped. "No. It wasn't a dig. Tonight, you're my beautiful, loving fiancee, and that's it. Tomorrow, I'll be sure to throw some digs your way, though. I don't want you getting spoiled."

Samantha had to laugh at that. "Deal."

"Now, take my arm and smile as we walk into the reception because your ex is staring at us from the doorway," Tucker said through gritted teeth with a smile plastered on his face.

"Thanks," she whispered as she slid her arm through his and smiled, pushing past Clark as they arrived at the reception.

THE SOUND of the music was almost deafening. Samantha sat at her assigned table with the other bridal party and their dates. Tucker sat beside her, his leg pressed against hers. It both bothered her and made her feel safe. She didn't like that at all. If there was one thing Samantha was proud of about herself, it was that she didn't need anyone else.

But she did.

"This steak is perfectly cooked, Katie. Who catered this?" Monica asked. This chick was always full of questions.

"Dolman's. They gave us an amazing deal."

"We'll have to get a quote from them for our wedding," Monica responded, smiling adoringly at Clark before shooting a quick glance at Samantha.

"Not us. We're going with a caterer in Atlanta. They do an amazing seafood spread. Right, sweetie?" Tucker said unexpectedly. He reached over and squeezed her hand.

"Right. Great lobster."

"Lobster? Isn't that a little pricey for a wedding? Or are you having a small event?" Monica asked, her bottom lip poked out a bit as if she was pitying them.

"Oh no. We're having a huge blowout with all of my friends, and of course Samantha's friends and clients from the city. We're thinking four hundred people, minimum."

Clark and Monica's eyes popped open, and

Samantha struggled not to laugh. Tucker was quick on his feet, she'd give him that much.

"Four hundred people?"

"Well, Samantha is a very popular attorney in Atlanta. But you know that already, Clark, right?"

Katie looked at her sister, her lips stitched together to stop her from laughing. Rick looked completely lost at first, but Katie leaned over to fill him in.

"Sure. Samantha has always been highly regarded in her field," Clark said begrudgingly.

Monica looked deflated and went back to eating her meal. Samantha honestly didn't know what her sister saw in this woman.

"So, where did you guys meet exactly?" Monica asked, directing her question at Samantha. Now it was her turn to make up some kind of believable story.

"Well, I came up to visit Katie last year, and Tucker was here…"

"That can't be right. Tucker just moved here a few weeks ago. And why does he live here and you live in Atlanta?" Clark asked.

Dang it. She'd totally forgotten that Tucker hadn't been living in Whiskey Ridge all that long.

"I was up here visiting. I love to camp in this area,

and Samantha ran into me at the coffee shop. Sparks flew, so to speak."

"And why the long distance romance?" Monica prodded.

"You know, this is Katie and Rick's night. Why are we focusing on us?" Samantha interjected.

"You're right. We're sorry, Katie and Rick," Clark said, keeping his eyes firmly on Samantha while he spoke. He knew something wasn't right.

"It's okay! We just want to thank everyone for helping so much with the wedding..." Katie said. Her voice trailed off in a muffled sound as Samantha's mind wandered. How was she going to get herself out of this mess?

It was only one night. Tomorrow, Clark would crawl off to wherever he lived now, and she'd only have Monica to deal with. Ugh. Monica wasn't going anywhere, and she'd surely report back to Clark. She had a whole month to dodge this woman while she would be housesitting for the newlyweds.

Suddenly, she felt Tucker take her hand. Not in a forceful way, just a light touch to let her know he was there. She smiled appreciatively at him before turning back to the table.

"So, when's the big day?" Monica asked, turning her attention back to Samantha.

"Everyday is a big day with this wonderful woman of mine. I couldn't believe she hadn't been snatched up by some other smart guy, but man is it my good fortune to have found her," Tucker said, leaning in and softly kissing the side of her neck.

Oh man, this was bad.

CHAPTER 7

"May I have this dance?" Tucker asked when the first slow song came on after the bride and groom's first dance. Samantha was thankful to have a reason to get up from the table and out of the line of fire.

Of course, Clark and Monica were hot on their heels, following them to the dance floor and standing so close that Samantha could practically touch them.

Tucker pulled her into an embrace, his arms around her waist. "How am I doing?" he whispered into her ear. Dang, he smelled good.

"I have to say that you're quite the thespian, Doctor Ellison." And he was quite a dancer too, it turned out.

"We almost got into some hot water over there, huh?"

"Yeah. I totally forgot you just moved here."

"Sorry about the kiss on the neck. I was just trying to…"

"I know. It's fine. I mean, we have to convince them, right?"

Tucker looked away and then back at her. "I don't get why they're so focused on us anyway? I mean, why do they care?"

"Clark has always been a bit controlling. Maybe he thought coming here was one upping me. He always hated my line of work, and the fact that I made more money than him."

"Ya know, you might need to come a little closer because right now we look like two eighth graders at a dance," Tucker said with a laugh.

Samantha stepped closer until they were touching as he pulled her even closer. It felt nice to be so close to a man again. And terrifying.

Without thinking - she blamed it on the romantic music - she pressed her cheek against his strong chest. And then she felt him wrap his arms around her tighter, one hand cradling the side of her head for a moment before trailing softly down her back. What was happening?

But she couldn't help it. Something just felt right in the moment. She needed to be close to him, and she didn't know why. It was all so confusing. This wasn't real. He was just acting, and he was a very good actor. She was just acting too. Wasn't she?

All she knew was that she wanted to stay here like this for another few hours, and that couldn't be good. Tomorrow couldn't come soon enough.

TUCKER SWAYED TO THE MUSIC, holding her tightly in his arms. Why was he doing this? Why did he care what her ex thought? Why did he want to hold her so tight that no one could find the separation between them?

This wasn't good for him. The divorce had left him shell shocked for so long, and he was only just now getting on his feet again. There had been days he didn't want to get out of bed. He'd felt like such a failure.

But Samantha needed him, and he was a sucker for a woman in need. He hated that part of himself. All they'd done since meeting was fight and argue and throw sarcastic comments around like a sexy game of dodgeball.

And yet he couldn't imagine being anywhere else right now.

He just wanted to protect her heart from this jerk named Clark. That guy was something else. After breaking up with her, why did he seem so intent on making her feel bad about herself?

Tucker decided not to pull at that string and instead focus on keeping the rhythm of the music. Right now he was thankful that his mother had forced him to take some ballroom dancing classes as a kid, although he was going to keep that little secret to himself.

Was that her heartbeat he felt against his abdomen? If so, she was as nervous as he was.

"You okay?" he asked. She tilted her head up, and immediately he regretted making her move.

"I am," she said, softer than he'd anticipated. She looked happy. Content. Peaceful. He hadn't seen that look on her before. It was stunning.

Tucker guided her head back to his chest and smiled before pressing his lips to the top of her head. He was going to regret this night. That much was sure.

His lips were on her head. They were warm. For a moment, she wanted to quickly look up and meet them before he could pull away. He was acting, she kept reminding herself.

Realizing her eyes had been closed, she opened them to see her sister smiling at her from across the dance floor. That knowing look that only sisters have made Samantha giggle.

"What are you laughing at?" Tucker asked.

Samantha looked up at him. He had the clearest blue eyes. Why hadn't she noticed that before? "Katie was smiling at me."

Tucker shot a glance in Katie's direction and chuckled. "I guess she's getting a big kick out of this."

"I'm sure."

"So, where's the adoring couple?" he asked as he looked around the dance floor. Clark and Monica were nowhere to be found.

"I don't know. Probably making out in a broom closet somewhere."

Tucker laughed. "Probably."

Samantha cleared her throat. "We don't have to keep dancing if you don't want to. I mean, you're probably tired from all the acting."

He smiled. "Right. We can take a break, if you want."

Samantha didn't know how to respond. She didn't really want a break, but she also didn't want to let her guard down. This was just a brief little acting job for Tucker, and she wasn't about to make anything more of it.

"Yeah. Let's get some punch."

They walked to the punch table, and Tucker filled two cups for them. Samantha carefully took a sip, trying not to spill anything on her dress.

"So, you're here for another month, right?"

"Yes. I promised to housesit for Katie and Rick. Of course, that was before I knew about Monica," she said with a laugh. "Now I have to spend a lot more time at the house so I can dodge her."

"I bet she'll just leave you alone once Clark goes back to whatever rock he crawled out from under." Tucker gulped down his punch and refilled it.

"Not a fan of Clark?"

"Are you?"

She laughed. "No. I used to be, a long time ago anyway."

"I don't see the attraction. Ya'll are nothing alike."

"Really? What do you mean?"

"He's a jerk, for one thing."

"I'm sure you thought I was a jerk for the last few days."

Tucker paused. "No. Not a jerk. Something else."

"What?"

"You want to get some air?" he said, obviously changing the subject.

"Sure." She followed him to the door, which he opened for her being the Southern gentleman that he was.

Thankfully, no one was outside so they took a seat on a bench under a gazebo.

"So what did you think about me?" she asked again.

"You don't forget, do you?"

"I'm an attorney. It's my job to remember."

"And to question," he said, chuckling.

"Don't deflect, Doctor Ellison."

"Okay. Fine. I thought at first that you were uptight. Snobby. Stuck up..."

"Got it. You aren't a fan."

"I wasn't finished. Never interrupt a witness. Isn't that a rule?"

"Nope, not even close."

"Anyway, then I thought you were hurt."

"Hurt?" She was almost offended at the insinuation, yet she also knew he was dead-on correct.

"I don't know, Sam. I just felt this sense of hurt or abandonment or loneliness..."

"I have a very full life in Atlanta, Tucker. I'm not lonely." She wondered if her nose was growing. The lies she was telling on this trip were not good. But there was no way she was letting on at how lonely she really was. She wasn't fessing up to the fact that she spent most nights working in her office eating Chinese take-out and watching everyone else live their lives through her large glass window over-looking the city.

"I don't doubt that. It was just a feeling I got."

"Well, not to worry. As soon as Katie and Rick get back from their honeymoon, I'll be back home living my life and all of this crap with Clark and Monica will be a distant memory."

Tucker smiled. "Right. Well, I guess we'd better get back in there."

"Of course," Samantha said. Why did she get the feeling that things had changed between them?

IT WAS VERY LATE, and Samantha could hardly keep her eyes open as Tucker drove them back toward the cabin. Night time in the Blue Ridge mountains was darker than any night in the city. The only thing she could see besides the headlights of the truck were the lightning bugs occasionally popping into view in the distance.

"You still awake?" Tucker asked. Samantha looked at the time. It was almost two in the morning.

"Barely." She leaned her head against the cold glass window and closed her eyes.

"That can't be comfortable," Tucker said, reaching over and gently pulling her head toward him. "I'm still your fake fiancé for the time being. Lay your head on my shoulder."

Samantha looked at him. "I'm fine. Really."

"Sam, humor me, okay? I'm afraid you'll get a concussion if I hit a pothole."

She smiled wearily before a yawn escaped her lips. "Fine." She laid her head down and that was all she remembered until the bumpiness of the gravel driveway woke her up.

The truck came to a stop, and Tucker turned off the lights. Samantha sat up, rubbing her eyes and inadvertently knocking one of her fake eyelashes off.

"Wow."

"What?" Tucker asked.

"It's so dark out here, but look at that moon. It's just breathtaking. So bright." She yanked off the other lash and stuffed them into her purse.

"You've seen the moon before, right?" Tucker asked with a laugh.

"Yeah, but it doesn't look like this in the city. It's just another light, mixed into all of the other distractions. It's like it's more beautiful here."

"I thought you loved the city?"

Samantha cleared her throat. "Of course I do. It's just different, that's all."

Tucker opened the door and walked around the truck. He pulled her door open at the same time she was attempting to open it, and down she fell into his arms.

"Shall I carry you over the threshold?" he asked with a nervous chuckle.

Samantha cleared her throat again, something she did when emotions got too much for her. "I think we should leave that to the newlyweds."

But the newlyweds were already long gone. They'd left the venue a couple of hours ago and caught a flight to start their honeymoon.

"Hey, Tucker?"

"Yeah?"

"Mind putting me down now?"

He smiled. "Right. Sorry."

He slowly lowered her to the ground.

"Well, thanks for being my pretend fiancé

tonight." She stepped back, unsure if she should shake his hand or what.

"No problem. But I am walking you inside, Sam."

"There's no need."

"It's dark and deserted out here. I want to check the place out."

"Oh come on. It's Whiskey Ridge!"

"Things can happen anywhere, Sam. You're an attorney. You know this."

He was right. And she hated that.

"Fine. But then that's it. I'm tired, and I want to go to bed."

"Trust me, so do I."

They stood there for another awkward moment before walking to the door. Samantha kicked off her heels as soon as they crossed the threshold.

"Not a fan of heels?" Tucker asked, shutting the door behind them as Sam turned on the foyer light.

"Actually, I wear them almost everyday at work."

"That's not what I asked you."

She turned and pursed her lips. "I actually hate them."

Tucker laughed. "Then why do you wear them?"

They made their way toward the kitchen as Samantha flipped on all of the lights. Sophie wiggled nervously in her large crate in the laundry room.

"Come on, girl," Samantha said as she opened the crate and then ran to the back door to let her out. "I wear them because that's what's expected of me in my line of work."

"People expect you to wear uncomfortable shoes?"

They walked out onto the darkened deck, only the bright light of the moon giving a glow to the yard as Sophie ran around looking for the perfect place to do her business.

"You ask the strangest questions, Tucker."

They sat down in the two log hewn chairs that overlooked the river below. "I'm just wondering why an intelligent woman would willingly wear something that hurt her feet just because other people expected it."

She thought for a moment. "Honestly, I have no idea. I just do."

"Hmm…"

"Hmm?"

"What other things do you do in your life because people expect it of you?"

"Jeez, what is up with you? Why are you trying to psychoanalyze me all of the sudden?"

Tucker leaned close to her ear, his breath trailing

down her neck. "Because I find you fascinating, Samantha Ryan."

Suddenly, it was like everything in her body lit up in a way she had a hard time describing. Her palms felt sweaty, her heart raced. Speaking in front of judges and juries didn't make her this nervous.

"I'm really not all that exciting, Tucker," she said, laughing nervously before standing up. "Come on, Sophie!"

Unbeknownst to her, he followed closely behind her as she walked to the top of the deck stairs to call the dog. When she turned back, they were practically nose to nose. She felt frozen in place, as if her legs had lead weights attached to them.

"Tucker," she said softly, their mouths literally an inch apart.

"Sam..."

Sometimes in life, there are moments that feel like slow motion, and this was one of those times. The only problem was the slow motion was her falling backwards down the wooden stairs as Sophie bumped her from behind as she came up the stairs. Tucker tried to react, but he wasn't quite fast enough and she found herself in a heap on the small concrete patio below.

"Owww...." was the only sound she could muster

as she laid on her side, bridesmaid dress askew, at the bottom of the stairs.

"Oh my God! Sam, I'm so sorry. I was standing too close…"

"I think I need to go to the ER," Samantha said through the pain.

"I'll call the ambulance…"

"No. Please. If you can get me to the truck, I'd rather go that way."

Tucker leaned crouched beside her. "What hurts?"

"My side and my head."

"Did you hit your head?" he asked, rubbing his hand carefully around her head.

"I don't really know. But I think I may have cracked a rib or something."

Tucker carefully slid his arms under her as she moaned in pain. He carried her up the stairs and placed her carefully on the sofa so he could put Sophie back in her cage and lock up the house.

Within minutes, he'd placed her in the truck and was speeding toward the only hospital in town.

TUCKER SAT beside Samantha in the small room. They'd given her something for the pain while they waited for the doctor to come back in. She looked peaceful as she slept, but the ride over had been hard on her. He saw tears escaping her eyes a few times, and he never wanted to see that again.

Something about this woman was driving him crazy. He wanted to know more about her. He wanted to help her. He wanted to spend every waking moment talking to her, and it was only getting worse. She didn't feel the same way, and he was in no position to get his heart broken all over again.

And yet he'd followed her so close to the edge of the stairs that he had basically caused her to fall when Sophie bumped her even slightly. He felt awful, and he didn't know how he'd ever make things right with her.

She stirred, so Tucker stood and walked over to her. The last thing he wanted was for her to wake up and think she was alone.

"Where am I?" she asked groggily. It was after four in the morning, after all.

"You're in the emergency room, remember?"

She looked around and rubbed her eyes. "Right. Ow." She reached for her left side and winced.

"Miss Ryan, you're up. How do you feel?"

"Bad." She was definitely a blunt woman.

"Well, you took quite a tumble. Cracked a rib or two, and you have a mild concussion."

"What do we do about my ribs?" she asked.

"Not a whole lot other than rest..." Tucker started to say. The doctor eyed him before turning back to Samantha.

"As your husband said, you'll need some good rest."

"Oh, he's not my husband," she said quickly. "Just a... friend."

For some reason, Tucker felt let down by that. At least it was better than saying he was her acquaintance. Being friends wasn't so bad, was it?

"Anyway, you'll need to be watched closely for at least twenty four hours. Your brain needs some time to recover. No TV and minimal activity for a few days. If you get any bad headaches, blurred vision... anything worrisome... you'll need to come back and see me. Okay?"

"But I'm housesitting for my sister. I have to take care of her dog..."

"The same dog that knocked you down the stairs?"

Samantha sighed. "Yes."

"You'll need some help until you recover, ma'am. You don't want to have a setback and end up back here, do you?"

"No."

"Good. I'm sure your friend here will be more than glad to help you recover. Am I right?" He looked at Tucker and smiled.

"Right," Tucker said, painting a smile on his face.

With that, the doctor swiftly left the room, and Tucker looked at Samantha.

"What am I going to do? I have to take care of Sophie for the next month, and I have big cases to work on when I get back…"

Tucker took her hands. "I'm going to help you, Sam. It's my fault, and I'm going to do everything I can to make it right."

"Your fault? What do you mean?"

"I snuck up behind you and was too close and…"

"Tucker, it was an accident. I don't blame you."

"Well, I blame me."

"Maybe don't say that to a lawyer," she said with a half hearted smile.

"Sue me if you must. I'd totally understand."

"I would sue Sophie before I'd sue you."

Tucker laughed. "Okay, then let's blame Sophie."

CHAPTER 8

*I*t was almost time for breakfast by the time they got back to the cabin. After picking up Samantha's medicine, Tucker had run into the grocery store to pick up supplies for breakfast.

"I'm carrying you," he said, as he stood beside the truck door.

"I can walk, Tucker. You don't need to carry me."

"Stop being hardheaded."

"Fine, but you're going to have a sore back and need medical assistance yourself."

"I'm willing to risk it."

He reached up and slid his arms under her as she put her arms around his neck. It felt good to be in his strong arms, something she didn't like admitting even to herself.

After getting her into bed, Tucker ran back to the truck for the groceries and then let Sophie out into the yard.

"I'm going to start breakfast. Let me know if you need anything. And don't worry, I'll keep Sophie away from you." He turned to go back up the hallway.

"Tucker?"

"Yes?"

"Thank you."

"You don't have to thank me, Sam. It's my fault."

She smiled. "I thought we were blaming the dog?"

He laughed and then walked up the hallway. This was going to be a long few days.

THE SMELL of bacon woke Samantha out of her stupor. She didn't know what drugs they'd given her at the hospital, but she needed them the next time insomnia hit her. She craned her head and looked at the small alarm clock on the nightstand. It was just after eight.

She reached for her cell phone, but knocked it

onto the floor, causing a loud noise. Suddenly, she heard metal crashing in the kitchen and hard footsteps approaching her room.

"Are you okay?" Tucker asked when he reached the doorway, a look of concern on his face.

Samantha giggled. "Yes. Sorry. I dropped my phone."

Tucker bent down and picked it up. "You don't need this, Sam. You need rest."

"I need bacon, actually."

Tucker smiled. "You smell that, huh?"

"It woke me up better than an alarm clock."

"Sorry about that. I just figured you might be hungry."

"I'm starving. But I do need to check my phone."

He pursed his lips. "Why?"

"Excuse me?"

"Why do you need to check your phone?"

"Because I have cases, Tucker. I have responsibilities that I can't just shirk."

He sighed. "Fine. But you have to agree to turn the phone off for the rest of the day."

"I'll turn it over, but not off."

"You're impossible."

"So I've been told," she said with as much of a

smile as she could muster. Everything in her body hurt.

Tucker handed her the phone. "Better go check the bacon."

Samantha looked at her phone. She had three voicemails and six text messages. Part of her wanted to turn it off and forget she was an attorney. Some days, it was all too much responsibility. She loved her job, but running her own large firm was exhausting. It left little time for a real life. She didn't travel or spend time with her friends much. Most nights, she was alone in her office until well after dinnertime, reviewing case files and answering emails.

"Eileen?"

"Sam? Thank goodness! I've been texting you since last night. We have some big issues on the Miller case. John totally dropped the ball…"

"Eileen…"

"Oh, and we got a continuance on the Salver Seafood case. Again. Ugh."

"Eileen…"

"And the file on the Lander case is missing. Did you take it with you?"

"Eileen!" Samantha yelled into the phone.

"What? Jeez, you just about burst my eardrum, Boss!"

"Stop talking."

"Okay," Eileen said softly.

"I had an accident last night. I spent the night in the ER."

"Oh no! What happened?"

Sam recounted the events of the last twenty four hours, including the wedding. When she was done, Eileen was quiet for once in her life.

"Is there anything I can do?" she finally asked, seriousness seeping into her words. And Eileen was rarely serious.

"No. I'm going to be fine. But I can't really work or look at my phone for a few days. Otherwise it could set back my recovery. So, have Lou take over my cases until I call you back next week, okay? He should be able to handle things."

Lou had been working for her for only a few months, but he was young and good at what he did. At least he could keep things moving until she got back.

"So, this guy… Tucker… he's going to watch out for you? Do you trust him?"

Samantha smiled to herself. "I do, actually."

"Hmmm… There's something in your voice… Do you like this guy?"

Samantha paused for a moment, choosing her words carefully as any good attorney would. "I'm only here for a month."

"That's not what I asked."

"But that's what I answered. Talk later," Samantha said with a smile before she pressed the end button.

Samantha slowly walked down the hallway. She wasn't supposed to be up walking around yet, but she was getting awfully bored lying in bed alone, staring at the prickly ceiling in her sister's guest bedroom. She held onto the wall for stability, not so much because of her head injury but because her ribcage ached in a way she couldn't describe.

"What are you doing out here?" Tucker asked, jumping up from the armchair where he was sitting watching some sporting event on TV.

"I'm getting a glass of water."

Tucker blocked her exit from the hallway and crossed his arms. "Back to bed, lady."

"I'm thirsty."

"Then you could've called for me."

"I didn't want to bother you."

"When has that stopped you before?" Tucker asked, a quirk of a smile on his face.

"Just let me get a bottle of water, and then I'll be out of your hair."

"Out of my hair?"

"Yes. I know how this works. A man likes to watch his sports crap alone."

Tucker looked at the TV and then back at her. "I'm not watching sports."

"I just saw it, Tucker. It's fine. I just need to get a water, and then I can go stare at the cobweb forming in the corner of my small bedroom."

Tucker chuckled. "First off, that was a news break that happened to include sports, which I don't actually watch. Secondly, I'll get your water." He turned and jogged to the kitchen.

"I'm so bored in there," Samantha whined.

"It's only been a few hours," Tucker said, handing her the bottle and turning her around to face the bedroom. "You'll survive, I promise."

"I don't handle boredom well." As she gingerly slid back into bed and opened the water bottle, Tucker stood in the doorway and smiled slightly. "What?"

"You really like to keep busy, don't you?"

"Yes. I can't do anything in here. I'm not tired anymore, and I'm going to go stir crazy in here."

"Well, I definitely don't want to see that side of you."

Samantha stared at him for a moment and then patted the bed next to her.

"What?"

"Sit. Please."

Tucker looked surprised and then uncomfortable. "Sam, I don't think we should…"

"Oh, be serious! I'm just looking for some company, and you're all I have in this whole town. Well, you and Sophie, but she almost killed me so we have some beef between us right now."

He smiled and slowly walked around the bed before sitting down. "So what do you want to do?"

"Well, we could talk, I guess."

"About?"

"Our lives. Our hopes and dreams. Pet peeves. That kind of thing."

"That sounds… terrible."

"Come on. Just play along."

"Fine. But I get to ask a question first."

Samantha nodded and leaned back against her pillow. "Ready."

"What is your biggest fear in life?"

She looked over at him and laughed. "Wow. That's a really serious question to start with!"

"Hey, it's your game."

"It's not a game, Tucker. It's called conversation."

"Okay, stop stalling. Is it a fear of snakes? Tight spaces? Monsters under the bed?"

She paused for a few moments. "Being alone."

Silence hung in the air for a few moments. "Being alone in what way?"

"No follow up questions in this game," she said, wagging her finger at him.

"I thought this wasn't a game?"

"My turn. Same question for you."

Tucker pursed his lips and thought a moment. "I'm a tough guy. No big fears here."

"Oh please," she said, rolling her eyes. "Don't think I didn't see you eyeing that spider on the deck the other day."

Tucker chuckled. "Well, they aren't my favorite insect. But they also aren't my biggest fear."

"So what is it?"

"I hate this game."

"Not a game," she said again.

"Okay, I would say my biggest fear is failure."

"Failure? What do you mean?"

"No follow up questions, ma'am," he said, putting his hand up. "My turn. What do you mean when you say you're afraid of being alone?"

Samantha rolled her eyes. "Maybe we should play Scrabble instead."

"Too intense. Plus, I would totally kick your butt at that game. Answer the question, please."

She took in a deep breath. "Fine. I worry that being so focused on my career will keep me from the other dreams I have for my life and that I will end up old and alone. There. Are you happy?"

Tucker looked at her, his face softer. "No. That doesn't make me happy, Sam."

"Why?"

"Because you deserve a great life. You shouldn't have to worry about ending up alone. Someone will come along and scoop you up."

She laughed. "Well, first I'd have to actually go on a date."

"Hey, you're already fake engaged, so you're well on your way to an actual date, right?"

"Right. So, let me ask you then… what failure are you afraid of?"

Tucker sighed. "I already failed at one marriage, and I'm afraid that maybe I won't get a second chance."

"You really want to be a family man, don't you?"

"I do."

"I can see that about you."

"Really?" Man, the way he smiled at her in that crooked way, one dimple taking over his right cheek, gave her chills.

"Yes. You'll be a great husband and father some day. You just have to meet the right woman."

"And you just have to meet the right guy. And be nice to him so you don't scare him off."

"Excuse me?" she said, sitting more upright in the bed, but not without causing the muscles around her ribcage to spasm. "Ouch!"

Tucker reached out and touched her side. "What happened?"

"I'm okay. I just sat up too fast." His hand lingered for a moment on her side before he pulled it away. "Now, what's this about scaring him off?"

"You're just a little… intimidating."

"No, I'm not."

"Sam, come on. You practically tore me limb from limb when we met."

"I was just having fun with you," she lied.

"Yeah, like a cat having fun with a chipmunk right before biting its head off."

"Yuck. Thanks for that image."

"I'm a vet. I've seen some things," he said with a laugh.

"I don't mean to be abrasive. I just have my guard up. Clark… and others… have made me a little wary, I guess."

"Do you like ice cream?" he asked.

"Wait, are we still playing?"

Tucker smiled. "No. I just wanted to know if you'd like some ice cream?"

"But we haven't had lunch yet."

Tucker leaned in close to her ear. "Be a rule-breaker."

Samantha struggled to get her bearings with his breath so close to her neck. "I like ice cream."

"Great. I'll go make us a couple of bowls."

TUCKER LEANED INTO THE FREEZER, letting the frigid air hit his face. Something needed to shock his system into realizing this whole thing was a very bad idea. He needed at least one whole room between them because sitting in the bed with her made him want to pull her close to him and wrap her in his arms.

Why did this have to happen? Why had he

pretended to be her fiancé? Why had he followed her to the steps and caused an accident that led him to this place?

If he'd just kept his mouth shut, none of this would be happening. And now, all he could think about was how scared she was to be alone.

That had nothing... nothing... to do with him. She wasn't the one. She was a high-powered, career-focused lawyer who didn't even live in Whiskey Ridge. He was a down-home guy who loved dogs and cats and all things country. This was all a recipe for disaster.

And yet, here he was scooping her a bowl of ice cream so they could eat in bed together. Maybe he needed his head examined.

"Okay, favorite eighties band?" Samantha asked as she stared up at the ceiling. Tucker laid beside her, their heads touching as he stared upward too.

"Bon Jovi, duh!"

"No! Duran Duran!" Samantha yelled.

Tucker laughed. "Can we agree they're both great?"

"Fine," she said. "But Duran Duran is better," she whispered under her breath.

"Favorite trip you've ever taken?" Tucker asked.

"Hawaii."

"Who'd you go with?"

"My Mom and my sister. We were just kids at the time, but I was amazed at the beauty. Have you ever been?"

"No, but I really want to go."

Samantha turned her head and looked at him. "What's holding you back? I mean, you only have to worry about yourself, and a successful veterinarian can definitely afford a nice trip to Hawaii."

"Well, Sam, what's holding me back is the fact that I don't want to go to one of the most beautiful and romantic places in the world alone."

She smiled sadly. "You'll find her, Tucker. You're too amazing to be alone for long."

Tucker sat up and faced her. "Did you just say I'm amazing?"

Samantha rolled her eyes. "Don't get a big head." She carefully eased up onto her elbows and then back against the pillow.

"I don't think you'd allow me to get a big head."

"True."

"So, we've been asking each other questions for two hours now. Did this cure your boredom?"

"Temporarily. I hate being stuck in the bed, especially when it's not even my bed."

"The doc said you could watch some TV. Want to join me on the sofa and watch a movie?"

"What kind of movie? Something bloody and gory?" Samantha asked, wrinkling her nose.

Tucker laughed. "Definitely not a chick flick."

"Excuse me, sir, but I don't even watch chick flicks. I prefer action adventure movies myself."

Tucker raised an eyebrow. "A woman after my own heart. Why don't we go see what's on demand? Maybe we can actually agree on something for once."

"Maybe," Samantha said cautiously. "But if you talk during the movie, I'll have to smack you."

TUCKER TRIED NOT to look at her too much, but it was hard. She was a beautiful woman with striking features, especially when she had her guard down. When she wasn't in full business mode or being mad about something, she had this serene look on her face. Peaceful. Happy. Calm.

He didn't dare say that to her. Being calm and peaceful wasn't something she seemed to relish. No, she seemed more content to appear strong and independent and totally without emotions.

It made him kind of sad.

But right now, he was exactly where he wanted to be. Sitting on one end of a cushy sofa, Samantha's socked feet firmly in his lap, watching an action movie. No woman he'd ever been with had wanted to watch an action movie. Not even his ex wife. It had always been chick flicks mixed with the occasional paranormal romance movie complete with cute vampires or sexy ghosts.

Sam was different. She was hard to unravel, though. She was like a large onion with a bunch of different layers, but before you could get to the good part, she made your eyes water like poison was thrown in them.

"Are you staring at me, Doctor Ellison?" she asked without breaking her gaze at the TV.

Tucker turned back to the screen. "No. I thought I saw a fly."

Samantha smiled, still looking at the movie, and for the first time since he was in high school, Tucker felt his face flush.

CHAPTER 9

The dull roar of the TV woke Samantha up. As she tried to open her eyes, she found it hard. Her head was pounding from the fall earlier, and her medicine had long since worn off.

Only the light of the TV flickering gave her a view of Tucker. He looked a little ethereal as he slept at the other end of the sofa. She pressed the info button on the remote and realized it was after midnight. They'd been piled up on the sofa for so long that they'd even slept straight through dinner.

After watching two whole movies and polishing off some popcorn as a snack, they'd fallen fast asleep. And Samantha felt comfortable, surprisingly.

Suddenly, and without warning, Sophie barked loudly and caused them both to jump. Tucker looked lost and confused for a moment before realizing where he was.

"What happened?"

"Sophie barked. I guess our nap exceeded the capacity of her bladder," Sam said. Poor Sophie had been locked up in the laundry room much of the day just to make sure she didn't knock Samantha down again.

Tucker stood up, stretched and walked over to let the dog out. Sophie ran straight past Samantha and out the back door.

"I guess she did have to go," Tucker said with a chuckle. "Man, I didn't know it was so late. When I get her back inside, I'll help you to bed."

"I think I'll just sleep out here," Samantha said.

"But you'll be uncomfortable."

"No. What's uncomfortable is sleeping in that hard bed back there. I don't know where my sister got it, but I think they sold torture chambers there. I'll get a lot more rest sleeping out here on this nice cushy sofa," she said with a grin as she rubbed the cushion next to her.

"Okay. Let me grab your blanket and pillow from the bed and we can switch places."

"Switch places?"

"Yeah. I'll take the torturous bed, and you can have the nice cushy sofa," Tucker said with a smile.

"You can't stay out here with me?" Samantha asked. Tucker froze in place for a moment.

"You want me to sleep out here with you?"

"I'm not really tired, actually. I thought maybe we could put on something funny and just wait for the sunrise."

"You're an unpredictable woman, Samantha Ryan."

She laughed. "I've been told that a few times in my life."

"I mean, one minute you can't wait to get away from me and then you want me to watch TV with you all night like we're kids having a slumber party." He sat on the coffee table across from her.

"Well, it has been a long time since I had a slumber party."

"We're not braiding each other's hair. That's where I draw the line," Tucker joked.

"So will you do it?"

"Of course. What kind of pretend fiancé would I be if I said no?"

She smiled. "Great! Lock that crazy dog back up and grab those doughnuts from the kitchen."

SHE WAS beautiful when she slept. Her features were softer, and that cute little smile that played on her face made him wonder what she was dreaming.

As the sun peeked through the blinds, Tucker mentally argued with himself. Why was he getting closer to this woman who wasn't his type at all? Why was he developing feelings for someone who hated Whiskey Ridge and was leaving in a few weeks?

Yet he couldn't stop staring at her. Their night of watching funny TV shows and stuffing their faces with doughnuts had left him more confused than ever.

And she snored. Softly, but it was definitely there. Should have been a turnoff, but it wasn't.

"What time is it?" Samantha asked groggily, her voice hoarse from sleep.

"Eight twenty," Tucker replied as he stretched his neck around in a circle. The sofa was comfortable for sitting, but definitely not for sleeping.

"Jeez, I'm sorry for keeping you here. Don't you need to work?"

"Don't worry. I texted my techs last night. I'm going in after lunch."

Samantha looked at him gratefully. "Thanks for taking care of me."

"It's been fun, surprisingly."

She smiled. "Yeah, it actually has been. But I need to get out of this house today." She sat up and stretched her arms out wide. "And I need a shower."

Tucker chuckled. "Can't really help you with that."

"No. You can't," she said as she slowly stood up. Tucker stood too, just in case she was still a little woozy. But she seemed fine, as if nothing had ever happened.

"I'll straighten up. Why don't you go get a nice, hot shower? I bet you'll feel good as new then."

Samantha nodded her head. "I bet you're right." She turned to walk up the hallway.

"And Sam?"

"Yeah?" she answered, turning back around.

Tucker stalled for a moment, unsure of why he even called her name. "I, uh, just wanted to say that I'm glad you're okay. Your clients need you."

What? Why had he said something so weird?

She smiled slightly. "Right. My clients." And then she rounded the corner to the bathroom.

136

SAMANTHA STOOD IN THE BATHROOM, looking at herself in the mirror. Gosh, she looked awful. Makeup worn off, hair a mess. She was almost embarrassed that Tucker had seen her this way.

What he'd said to her in the hallway lingered in her mind and bothered her more than she'd want to admit. Her clients? As if they were the only ones who needed her?

And then she thought about it. Who else really did need her? Maybe her sister, but that was it. And even she had a husband now.

Her eyes watered as she realized that she really had no one who needed her. Just the people that were paying her for her legal services, and even that was replaceable. They could find an attorney anywhere.

She sat down on the edge of the tub and allowed a stray tear to fall. What had become of her life? Had she been so blind that she'd allowed her life to become all about work and money and achievement? Where was the balance everyone talked about?

She had no one to go home to. No one to rub her shoulders after a long day at work. No one to sit by the fire with on cold winter nights. No one to watch the sun set or the sun rise. No one who wanted to merge bank accounts and DVD collections.

She was alone.

The thought hit her like a ton of bricks. And while she wanted to believe this was all brought on by the romance of her sister's wedding, she knew it wasn't. She'd long been bottling up these feelings of loneliness, and now they were smacking her straight in the face.

Even watching Clark and Monica made her jealous. What was it like to wake up in the morning and see the same face everyday? The face of the person she'd spend the rest of her life with?

What was it like to be the bride and not always the bridesmaid?

Ugh. She hated when she fell into the hole of dark thoughts. In reality, she was living the life a lot of people dreamed of. Plenty of money. A successful career. A killer apartment overlooking the city. A nice car with heated seats.

But it all seemed so empty lately. Her soul longed for more, and maybe that was selfish when so many people had so little. Even in Whiskey Ridge, there were lots of people who didn't have anywhere near the material wealth that she did, yet they seemed happier. More fulfilled.

She stood up and looked in the mirror at herself. For the first time in a long time, she saw the unvarnished version of Samantha looking back at her. Not the made up, fake version that she presented to her clients. Not the bulldog, steely determination face she made when her competition stood in front of her.

No, this was just Sam. And that was both scary and invigorating to her. In Whiskey Ridge, she could just be herself. Even if that only lasted for another three weeks or so, she was going to take advantage of it and find out who she really was once and for all.

THE NEXT COUPLE of days consisted of Samantha getting back to regular life. Well, whatever that meant when she wasn't living in her own space.

Her sister had texted how much fun they were having on their honeymoon. Samantha was happy for Katie yet envious at the same time.

Tucker had been checking in on her frequently. Sometimes he would drive over on his lunch break just to make sure she was alright. Her ribs still hurt when she moved wrong, but for the most part she was back to normal within two days of tumbling down the stairs.

She'd had a long talk with Sophie, who seemed to be settling into her new routine too.

Samantha stood in the kitchen of her sister's cabin and surveyed her surroundings. It was a nice place, although a bit more rustic than she normally liked. Still, the place had a homey feel. It was nice to be away from the sounds and smells of the big city. The more she was away, the less she missed it, a fact that shocked her to her core.

She smeared mayo on some bread and slapped a piece of ham on it before sliding it onto a small white plate. She decided she had to go grocery shopping soon or else risk starvation. This elementary school cafeteria diet she was eating wasn't what she was used to at all. She missed Andre, her personal chef.

"Knock knock." Tucker rarely actually knocked on the door. He just poked his head in the back door and yelled the words.

"I've got to start locking that door," Sam called back as Sophie sprinted past her and jumped up on Tucker's side.

"Yeah, I'm a real threat. How's the patient?"

"I'm not a patient anymore. I'm perfectly fine." She took a bite out of her sandwich and smiled.

"Good, because I'm here to drag you out of this cabin to have some fun. Now, put that juvenile, fairly disgusting, sandwich of yours away and grab your shoes."

Samantha stared at him for a moment. "Where are we going?"

"Just wear something you don't mind getting wet."

"Excuse me?"

Tucker sat down across from her. "Do you trust me?"

"Only slightly," she replied with a grin.

"That's good enough. Wear sneakers," he said before getting up and grabbing a couple of water bottles.

"I don't like surprises, Tucker."

"Trust me, Miss Ryan..." he called from the refrigerator. "And also, you really need to go to the grocery store."

Samantha walked down the hall to get her shoes. "Oh, I'm sorry, I was busy bonking my head."

Tucker laughed. "You should really be more careful. You might break a hip next time."

She was starting to love their constant banter.

"Are you calling me old?" Samantha said from right behind him, causing Tucker to jump a bit.

"Jeez!"

"Yeah, it's startling when someone walks up right behind you, isn't it?" she teased.

"I feel guilty enough."

"Don't feel guilty, Tucker. I'm just joking."

"Okay, let's go," he said as he struggled to hold the water bottles and some snacks he'd grabbed from the pantry. Samantha pulled out a reusable shopping bag and he tossed them in.

"Fine. But if this results in another ER visit, I'm suing you. I know a very good lawyer, you know."

"Noted."

CHAPTER 10

*A*s they drove down the long gravel road, Samantha wondered where they were going. She'd never really been an outdoorsy gal, but she had to admit this area was beautiful. With huge trees surrounding them on all sides, and the blue tinged mountains dotting the landscape around them, she felt peaceful. Safe. Calm. It was both soothing and scary at the same time.

"Here we are," Tucker said, as he pulled down a steep, rocky driveway and stopped the truck. Sam looked around.

"We're nowhere, Tucker. Literally. There's nothing here."

"Oh yes there is. Come on. And grab the bag."

She opened her door to find him already

standing there waiting to help her down. Her ribs were still sore, so she carefully stepped down onto the leaf covered ground below.

"Careful…"

"I feel like I'm going to fall."

"I won't let you fall again, Sam. Never." The way he said it made her tingly all over. She believed him more than she'd ever believed anyone in her life.

Once they were out of the truck, Tucker led them down a narrow path. It seemed to go straight downhill. She could hear water in the distance.

After pushing back a stray tree limb so they could walk under, the landscape gave way to the most picturesque scene. The river, calm and serene, flowed before them. Jagged rocks, some that soared high above them, surrounded the water. And beside the shore was a canoe built for two.

Samantha smiled. "We're going canoeing?"

"Yep. You ever been?"

"No, I haven't. I always thought I'd do it in Venice, though."

"Well, Whiskey Ridge is better than Venice, if you ask me."

"Oh yeah?"

"No pesky American tourists," Tucker said with a smile.

"True."

"Come on." He held out his hand. She took it, unwilling to fall again and risk a major injury this time. The leaves were slick from overnight rain, and she almost fell in before they could get to the canoe.

Tucker eased it into the water and helped Samantha inside before joining her. He pushed it off into the water, and they immediately started moving.

"How will we get back to the truck?"

"Don't worry, Sam. I've got this."

"Who's canoe is this?"

"Mine." He used the oars to move them further down the river.

"Who's property is this?"

"My uncle's. You're full of questions."

Samantha laughed. "Sorry. It's a symptom of the job I do everyday."

"Do you like your work?"

"I love it."

"What do you love about it?" Tucker asked as he took a break from rowing for a bit and let them float along the calm water. It was really more of a large creek than part of the river, she realized.

"I love helping people get what they deserve. I believe in fairness and doing what's right, so I get to help people fight for that everyday. What about you? Do you love your job?"

A smile spread across his face. "You know I adore my job. I'd do it for free."

"Really? I don't know if I'd say that about my career."

"I love animals. Anything I can do to help them is a privilege to me."

"Do you plan to stay here forever?"

Tucker chuckled. "You act like this is a step down or something, Sam."

"I didn't mean it that way."

"I think you did, actually. And that's okay. You just haven't seen it yet."

She cocked her head to the side. "Seen what?"

"The reason people stay here," he said, the corners of his mouth turning up into a smile. He had dimples that made her swoon a bit.

"And what is that reason?"

"It's different for everybody, I guess. Some people come here because their family is here. Others come because they want to get away from the hectic pace of city life. You have to find your own reason."

Samantha laughed. "I don't need a reason because I'm not staying, Tucker. Remember?"

He looked at her for a moment before making an almost imperceptible sound. "Right."

"You think I'm staying here? Seriously? Why would I do that? My whole life and business is in Atlanta."

"Never say never, Sam. Whiskey Ridge has a way of changing folks."

She shook her head and chuckled. As she looked around at the scenery, she had to admit it was breathtaking. The sky was so blue today that there wasn't a cloud to be found anywhere. And the water below them was surprisingly clear. She could even see the fish swimming around them.

"My family used to come camping here when I was a kid. I remember fishing off that old dock over there." Samantha looked at where he was pointing, but all that remained was a ramshackle structure that could no longer be called a dock. "We stopped coming when I was twelve."

"Why'd you stop coming?" Samantha asked as she dug through the bag looking for a snack. Since he'd snatched her sandwich away, she was starving.

"That's when we lost my sister, Janie."

Samantha stilled in her seat. He wasn't looking at her. Instead, he was staring at the decrepit little dock.

"I'm so sorry, Tucker. How old was she?"

"Fourteen."

"Wow. Do you mind if I ask what happened?"

He took in a deep breath and blew it out. "She was riding her bike over a bridge near our house. Drunk driver hit her, and it threw her into the lake below. Took them two days to find her body."

Samantha's stomach churned. She didn't know what to say. The pain in Tucker's eyes was almost unbearable to see.

"Oh, Tucker, I can't imagine what that was like for you and your parents."

"After we lost her, they couldn't bear to come back to Whiskey Ridge. Camping together was a huge part of our family, and we'd just gotten home the day before. So this place brought back a lot of good memories that were just too painful for them."

"So why did you decide to move here?"

"Janie was my reason. This was the last place we made memories together as brother and sister. Moving here and giving back to this community she loved keeps me close to her. She loved animals, especially dogs. She'd gotten a puppy for her fourteenth birthday. Named him Fluffy McFlufferson, or Fluff for short," he said with a smile. "I took care of him until he died when I was twenty-one."

Instinctively, Samantha reached over and touched his hand as it rested on the side of the canoe. Tucker looked at her, an appreciative smile on his face.

"It was a long time ago."

"But I know the pain never goes away."

He squeezed her hand before letting it go. "True. I miss her everyday."

Samantha felt the loss of his hand. She hadn't wanted him to let her hand go, a thought which made her uncomfortable.

They continued moving down the still waters until Tucker steered the canoe toward the side of a little inlet.

He grabbed hold of a tree root and pulled the canoe to shore before tying it off to the same root.

"Where are we?"

"I want to show you something," he said as he stood up and stepped out onto the grassy spot. He reached a hand down to Sam, and she slowly pulled herself up, being careful not to wrench her side all over again. "Follow me."

She followed behind him, trying in vain not to notice how great his butt looked in the jeans he was wearing. What was wrong with her? Obviously, she needed to date more or something.

"Look," he said, pointing ahead to a clearing that was just steps from the water.

"It's beautiful land. What is this place?"

"It's my lot. I bought it a few weeks ago, and construction starts on my house next month." The pride he felt was evident on his face.

"Oh, Tucker, it's gorgeous. You're going to love it here, I'm sure."

He looked at her for a moment and swallowed, as if he was thinking something but didn't want to say it.

"Yeah, I'm looking forward to it. Of course, I'm going to have to hire a decorator so this place doesn't look like a seventies bachelor pad or something."

Samantha laughed. "I can help you if you want."

"You won't be here, Sam. Remember?"

She took in a breath. "Right. Well, you can email me or text me photos…"

"Sure."

A moment of silence hung between them. Samantha didn't know why she felt a sadness, almost, at the thought of him building a house there.

"You know, there's a great website about home decorat…" Samantha started to say, but a rogue wasp buzzed by them and landed on her chest. Given that she was terrified of any flying insect, especially one that could sting her, she ran in a circle swatting her hands in the air before running directly into Tucker's arms and pressing herself to his chest.

"It's okay, Sam," he said with a laugh. She didn't move. She didn't know why she didn't move. She just didn't. It felt good to be there in his arms. It felt safe and warm and right. And she just stood there like an idiot, her cheek pressed to his firm chest.

And just as she was about to pull away and apologize profusely for acting like a six year old, Tucker wrapped his arms around her.

It was a familiar embrace, like two people who'd been together forever. It felt like two halves of a whole. Her eyes began to water as emotions erupted just under the surface.

She stood there, wrapped in his arms, confused and full of questions. Why wasn't he pulling away? Why wasn't she? What did he think of her right now? Did he think she was weak? Damaged in some way? Why was he holding her so close? Was he just trying to be a friend?

One of his hands trailed up her back and stroked the back of her head before pressing his lips to the top of her head.

She wrapped her arms around him instinctively,

still unsure of what any of this meant. It couldn't mean anything anyway. She was going back to Atlanta soon, and even though Whiskey Ridge was just a couple of hours away, she wasn't into long distance relationships. Lately, she wasn't into relationships at all.

"You okay?" Tucker finally asked softly. Maybe he was just trying to comfort her from the wasp sighting. Still, it was a bit of overkill to hold her so close and kiss her head because of a wasp.

What was she to say? "Yes, I'm fine but please keep holding me close because I like it. Oh, and your butt looks awesome in those jeans."

Instead, she just said, "I'm okay."

And then she felt a cool breeze between them as Tucker pulled away slightly. His arms were still on her shoulders, though, as he looked down at her.

She hadn't seen this look in his eyes before, the one that came just before two people kissed. Time stood still as he tilted her chin up to look at him. Why was she so nervous?

"I really, really want to kiss you right now," he said softly. "But I don't think I can."

"Okay…" she said, not knowing what she really wanted to say other than *"Yes, please kiss me and put me out of my misery"*.

"Do you want me to kiss you, Sam?" Oh crap, he actually asked. Now what?

"I, um…"

"Excuse me, sir?" a man called from the other side of the lot. He was on some kind of tractor. Tucker sighed and dropped his hands to his sides.

"You've got to be kidding me," he mumbled as he looked over at the man. "How can I help you?" Tucker called back. The man waved him over. "I'll be right back, okay?"

Samantha nodded and watched him walk away. What had just happened? She was so confused on what he felt, but even more so on what she felt.

This was stupid. She was going home in a few weeks. She was only housesitting. They were two totally different people, weren't they? He liked rivers and creeks. She liked the blue waters of Greece. The only problem was she was sort of liking the rivers and creeks around Whiskey Ridge too. And no matter how many times she internally recited all of the reasons they couldn't be together, the reasons never seemed valid enough.

What was happening to her?

"Sorry about that," Tucker said as he made his way through the thick brush. "Turns out he was here to start clearing the land."

"Isn't it earlier than you expected?"

"Yeah, who knew contractors could actually do things early?" he said with a nervous laugh. "So I guess we'd better head back to the canoe before we get dirt thrown on us."

"Wouldn't be the first time for me," Samantha said with a giggle as they walked.

"What?"

"Yeah, I had this very contentious case once over a piece of property. It was three brothers all fighting for a freaking acre of land. An acre! Ridiculous. But one of them got combative, and I ended up with lovely Georgia red clay all over my favorite white pantsuit."

Tucker helped her into the canoe before untying it and climbing inside. "So what did you do then?"

Samantha smiled slyly. "I may have poured some water on some of the dirt and returned it as mud."

"You did not!"

"I'm not proud of it… Well, I am a little proud of it!"

"You're amazing," Tucker said as he rowed them out into the open water again.

"What?"

"I said you're amazing, Sam."

"I'm really not."

"Yes, you are. You have this big career where you help people get justice. That's pretty cool if you ask me."

She leaned over the side of the boat and looked into the water. "Is this water clean?"

"What?"

"Like, if I jumped into it, would I die of a parasite?"

Tucker laughed out loud. "No, you wouldn't die. Mountain water is clean, at least around here…"

Before Tucker could finish his sentence, and without thinking it through, Samantha rolled over the side of the canoe and into the water. It was cold, something she wasn't expecting. And it was deeper than she thought, coming up to her mid chest.

"Are you crazy?" Tucker asked as he struggled to catch his breath from laughing so hard.

"I think so! It's so freaking cold!"

"I could have told you that!"

"Are you too scared to join me?" she taunted.

"I'm not scared. I'm just not nuts!"

"Oh come on, Doctor Ellison. Don't be such a stick in the mud!"

"Stick in the mud, huh?" He pulled off his outer shirt, revealing just a white t-shirt underneath, and tossed it aside before sliding into the water next to her, jeans and all.

Samantha had never felt so free. Floating in the middle of a random little creek in the mountains of north Georgia had made her feel alive and spontaneous again.

"Man, this *is* cold!" Tucker said.

"Yeah, I didn't think it would be so cold this time of the year." It was the tail end of summer and not quite fall, but the water felt like it was the middle of winter.

"Mountain water is pretty much always cold," he said with a smile. "You look so different."

"Different how? You mean because I'm wet?"

He smiled. "No, because you're happy. Like, I think I see joy on your face right now." He reached out and touched her cheek.

"And? How does it look?"

"Irresistible," he said, pulling her forward to meet him. His lips met hers, soft at first, and then more forceful, but in a good way. She wrapped her arms around his neck and her legs around his waist, their kisses growing more passionate with each passing second. She'd never been kissed like this, and she never wanted it to end.

But then she saw the canoe floating away and

thought that might be an important detail to mention.

"Tucker…" she said breathlessly.

"What?"

"It's getting away…" she said between his lips pressing into hers over and over again.

"You mean this situation is getting away from us?" he asked.

"No! The canoe is getting away from us, silly!"

Tucker turned to see their only source of transportation floating down the stream. "Oh, crap! Wait here!"

He swam quickly over and grabbed the rope, trying in vain to pull it back toward Sam. The current was weak, but still too strong to do that so Sam swam to him.

He tied it to another tree that had lowhanging limbs. "Want to climb up?"

"Sure," she said, wondering if her ribs were going to allow it. Surprisingly she was able to climb up with the help of Tucker's hand on her rear end, a feeling she didn't mind at all.

They sat on the thick limb for a few moments, each of them catching their breath from the swim.

"Sorry about that," Tucker finally said.

"It's okay. It was just a momentary lapse of judgment on both of our parts. I mean, I'm leaving in a few weeks. And let's face it, we aren't exactly a match made in heaven, are we?"

Tucker's expression fell flat. He chuckled half heartedly. "I was referring to the fact that I let the canoe float away."

Sam's stomach lurched into her chest. Why had she just said those things? She didn't even know if she meant them, and now he looked completely confused and maybe even a little sad. She was her own worst enemy sometimes. How was it that she was so good at fighting in court and so terribly bad at the emotional stuff that came along with just being human?

"I guess I stuck my foot in my mouth," she said softly. "Look, Tucker, I…"

"No," he said, holding up his hand. "It's okay, Sam. You've made yourself perfectly clear the whole time you've been here. I shouldn't have assumed…"

"But, I…"

"Please. This is embarrassing enough. Can we just not talk about it anymore?" His face was actually turning a little red, which was cute but also made her sad.

"Okay."

"Maybe we should head back?" He wasn't looking at her now.

"Okay," she said again. Words were failing her right now. As verbose as she was in her law career, finding the right words when it came to Tucker was proving to be a lot more difficult. All she knew right now was she felt a deep loss in the center of her soul, and she wasn't sure how to repair it.

They quietly climbed back into the canoe and made their way toward the cabin without another word spoken. Never had silence been so loud.

CHAPTER 11

$\mathcal{T}$ucker sat at his desk reviewing patient files, but his mind just wasn't in it today. He hadn't seen Sam in three days after the embarrassing incident in the river. Why had he thought he could kiss her? He blamed himself. He'd cornered her, made her feel like she had to do something she obviously hadn't wanted to do. He felt horrible.

But she had wrapped her legs around his waist, and that was something, wasn't it? Maybe she was having a hard time staying afloat in the water, he decided, although he didn't really believe it.

He'd texted her once a day just to make sure she was okay with her head and ribs. And he had to admit a small part of him just wanted to know if she'd respond, which she always did.

But now he didn't know where to go with their friendship. Should he invite her to dinner? Steer clear until her sister came back? After all, he'd done his duty making sure she was okay. He wasn't responsible for her. She was an adult.

"Doctor Ellison? Your three o'clock is here."

"I'll be there in a second," he said a little too snippily. The vet tech looked stunned. "Sorry. I didn't get much sleep last night."

"Okay..." she said softly as she closed his office door. What was this woman doing to him? It was ridiculous. He wasn't a kid anymore. He couldn't let his business suffer over some woman who was going home soon.

In that moment, Tucker made the decision to just stay clear of Samantha Ryan. It was the best choice for both of them. He was officially breaking up with his fake fiancee and moving on with his life.

SAMANTHA STOOD in front of the coffee shop, trying to decide if she should go in. She'd done her best to avoid Monica, but that was mainly because she was stuck at home recovering from her fall. Now that she felt back to normal for the most part, she had to get out of the cabin for awhile.

Tucker had texted her once a day, mainly just checking that she was okay and didn't need anything. But she was sad that they weren't really talking. She missed that already, which was shocking to her in a way.

Still, maybe it was better that they got used to being apart. She was going home in a few weeks, and she'd need a little distance to get over that kiss. She hadn't stopped thinking about it yet.

She sat down at one of the bistro tables outside of the coffee shop and took a deep breath of the mountain air. It was so crisp in Whiskey Ridge. She had never really understood what "crisp" meant until she'd come here, and that was the only good way to describe it. It felt clean and new everyday, unlike the "interesting" smells of the big city.

"Can I help you, hon?" the server asked. She hadn't even realized the servers came outside to take orders.

"Oh. Sure. I'll take a latte, extra sugar, please."

"Be right back."

Samantha looked down at her phone, supposedly checking it for work related messages, but actually hoping that Tucker had texted her. Maybe to invite her to lunch? Maybe offering another kiss?

She was an idiot. Why was she pining for this guy? It had to be the mountain air affecting her senses. She was no longer the cutthroat attorney that everyone feared. In Whiskey Ridge, she was a woman who just wanted to be with a man who liked her. She wanted to snuggle her head against his chest and take in the smell of him. She was weak.

To Samantha, showing emotions had always been hard. It made her feel way too vulnerable, and Tucker had done just that. Made her mad, at times. Made her feel protected at other times. It was all so confusing.

It was one of the ways that she and her sister were so different. Katie was all about feelings and showing them to everyone she met. She was a hugger, a cheek kisser and the first one to offer a big, cheesy grin in just about any situation. Samantha was far more reserved, shielding her heart more and more every time a relationship failed.

"Well, well, well. Look who I found this morning." Oh no. She looked up to see Clark standing there, coffee in hand. He'd been inside the coffee shop the whole time.

"Clark. What are you still doing here?"

"I guess I forgot to tell you. I'm staying in Whiskey Ridge for the foreseeable future."

"What? Why?"

"Well, for one thing, I have a wedding to plan. Much like you, right?" The look on his face was snide, as if he didn't believe her story of being engaged to Tucker. She hated when people thought they had something on her. It brought out that cutthroat side again. Maybe she should just 'fess up and admit she wasn't engaged. No, she couldn't do that. She'd rather step in front of a speeding bus before admitting to her big fat lie.

"Right. Deep in wedding planning over here too."

Clark looked around. "So where is your fiancé anyway?"

Sam smiled. "At work. And where is your beloved?"

"Teaching an afternoon yoga class."

"Oh right. Yoga," Samantha said, rolling her eyes. She wasn't sure why she rolled her eyes. She liked yoga and took a class in Atlanta three times a week. She just didn't like this particular yoga teacher.

"So, have you decided when the big day is?" Clark asked as he sat down in the other chair.

Samantha leaned across the table. "Clark, you

seem a little preoccupied with my private affairs. Is there a reason for that?"

He chuckled under his breath. "Come on, Sam. I know you too well. When are you just going to come clean?"

"Come clean about what?" The server returned with her latte, thankfully in a takeout cup. Sam quickly handed her some cash and stood up. Unfortunately, Clark followed her.

"You know what I mean, Sam. I'm really trying not to embarrass you."

She stopped at the end of the sidewalk and turned around. "Embarrass me? Clark, you're embarrassing yourself. Why are you following me?"

He shook his head. "We both know you aren't engaged, Sam. You and that Tucker guy must have worked out some deal..."

"What makes you think I'd do a thing like that? Do I seem like a desperate woman to you?"

"To be honest, yes."

Samantha was fuming mad. She could feel the anger rising within her, and she clenched her fist at her side, careful not to clinch the other one and end up with burns all over her hand from the hot coffee.

"If I didn't care about getting a felony on my record, I'd clock you right now!"

Clark held his hands up and stepped back. "Calm down."

"Don't you tell me to calm down, Clark. You just accused me of pretending to have a fiancé. And for what? To impress you?"

"Maybe. I mean, I could tell you were surprised to see me here. I think you just made all of this up to get back at me. Or to save face? It's really beneath you, Sam."

"No, Clark. You're beneath me. Under my heel. So far in the past that you're barely a blip on the history of my life."

"Yikes. You seem really upset about this. But what I don't hear are words about how much you love this Tucker guy. Why is that? Could it be because you don't love him?"

She took in a deep breath. "Maybe it's because I don't care to share my innermost thoughts and feelings with a guy who seems intent on being a royal jerk face. But, just to humor you I will say that I adore Tucker. He's the best man I've ever met. He's protective, and he feels safe. I want to be with him because no one else could ever compare. Oh, and he's the best kisser I've ever dated. Sorry, but you don't even rank in the top three. Good luck to

Monica. It was like kissing a lizard..." she mumbled, her words trailing off.

Clark pursed his lips and sucked a breath through his nose, his nostrils flaring like two butterfly wings.

"I'd hoped you would just come clean..."

"Oh, hey, sweetie. There you are..." Sam turned to see Tucker walking out from behind a building next to where they'd been talking. Oh, no. How much had he heard?

"Tucker," Clark said simply.

"Craig," Tucker said back.

"It's Clark, actually."

"Oh, sorry," Tucker said, looking at Sam. She could tell he was trying not to laugh. "I missed you this morning," he said before pulling her into a passionate kiss. This one was far beyond what happened at the river, and Sam literally felt weak in the knees as he carefully leaned her back.

"Really? Is this necessary?" Clark finally said. Tucker stood Sam up and grinned.

"Well, when you're in love, you just can't help it sometimes, right?"

Clark rolled his eyes. "I have a conference call."

"See ya, Craig!" Tucker called after Clark as he walked away.

Tucker pulled Sam behind the building before they both broke out in hysterics.

"Oh my gosh, the look on his face…" Sam said, tears rolling down her cheeks. "Thank you! I was within seconds of decking him."

"Yeah, he's a piece of work. I heard the whole thing."

Sam took in a breath. "The whole thing?"

"You're quite the actress. Do you do community theater?"

"Very funny."

"I almost believed it."

"Which part?"

Tucker leaned against the brick wall. "The part where you said you adored me and I make you feel safe and protected."

Samantha smiled. "All of that was true, Tucker."

"What?"

"Look, if I lived here and things were different…"

He smiled sadly. "I get it. And you're right. But I've missed hanging out with you these last few days, so can we at least do that? I don't have a lot of friends here yet, and for some reason you don't irritate me like you used to."

"Back at ya," Sam said with a laugh.

"And since it looks like Clark is here to stay for awhile, you still need a fake fiancé, right?"

"Right…"

"So how about we throw caution to the wind, play our roles really good in public and just have fun for the next two and a half weeks?"

"And then?"

"Then we go our separate ways, maybe text once in a while, and you buy me dinner if I ever get lost and end up in the godforsaken city."

"Deal."

"So let me get this straight. You and this handsome vet are going to keep pretending you're engaged until you leave in a couple of weeks?" Eileen asked during their daily phone call.

Samantha sighed. "Yeah."

"Was that a sign of irritation or of pleasure?"

"Maybe a little of both…"

"Boss, you seem different."

"How so?"

"Well, for one thing, we've been on the phone for ten minutes and you haven't asked me one work related question. But you have recounted every moment spent with Tucker since the last time we spoke."

She wanted to argue, but she couldn't because that was totally true. In fact, she hadn't thought a bit about work all day. Instead, she'd spent the day walking around the square in Whiskey Ridge with Tucker. They'd shared an ice cream, eaten sandwiches by the riverwalk and even had one of those old time pictures taken that looked like they were in the 1860's.

"Can I ask you one glaring question, Boss?"

"What's that?"

"Correct me if I'm wrong, but won't Clark know that this whole thing was a lie when you go back to Atlanta and leave Tucker in the dust?"

Samantha didn't like to think about that part of it. She was keenly aware that was a big problem in this whole setup, but neither she nor Tucker would address it. They just wanted to have fun together, but the thought of going home and letting Clark realize he was right all along made her stomach churn.

"I don't know yet. I'll cross that bridge when I get to it."

"Sweetie, that bridge is already on fire, and there isn't enough water in all of Georgia to put it out."

"Your metaphors never make any sense. You know that, right?" Samantha asked with a laugh.

"Whatever. I'll talk to you tomorrow."

"Wait! What about the file updates?"

"Sam, enjoy your time. Fake fiancés don't come along every day. I'll call you tomorrow."

"How's your steak?" Tucker asked as they sat at the kitchen table. Samantha seemed distracted tonight, which wasn't like her. Lately, she'd been fun and spontaneous, but she didn't act like that tonight.

"It's good. Cooked perfectly." She smiled appreciatively and took another bite.

"Are you okay?"

She sighed and shrugged her shoulders. "I'm fine. Just a lot on my mind."

"Such as?"

"It's nothing, really."

"Sam…"

"Fine. I spoke to my assistant yesterday, and it got me thinking."

"About a case?"

"No. About this whole situation. I think I should just come clean to Clark and get it over with."

"Are you kidding me?"

"No."

"Why would you do that?"

"Well, first of all, this whole lie has been so juvenile. I shouldn't care what he thinks of me. His opinion about my life doesn't matter."

"True."

"And second, there's no good way out of this mess. When I leave to go back to Atlanta and you're still here, he's going to know."

"Not necessarily. We can say you went home to wrap up some cases."

"And then what, Tucker? Then we actually plan a fake wedding and have a fake ceremony and a couple of fake kids? We can buy some of those realistic looking baby dolls and push them around town in expensive strollers."

Tucker smiled. "Okay, but can we have three fake kids? I've always wanted three."

"Very funny."

"Why is this all dawning on you now, Sam?"

"I told you. Because my assistant brought it up."

"And because you saw Clark the other day?"

"That man just grates on my last nerve," she said as she stood up to refill her glass of wine.

"Hey, you're the one who dated him."

Sam looked at Tucker, who was shrugging his shoulders like a little kid. "I know, right? What was I thinking." She slid back into her chair and put her head in her hands. "Ugh."

"How about we don't think that far ahead? Maybe Clark will leave on some unexpected business trip before you have to leave. Or maybe he turns up missing…"

"Tucker!"

"I'm just playing pretend…"

"You're a goofball. But this isn't funny," she whined as she pressed her forehead to the table.

Tucker reached across and rubbed her shoulder. "Look, was this a dumb plan from the beginning? Yes. Has it been fun to aggravate your ex? Yes."

Samantha sat up and cocked her head. "And what does any of that have to do with this?"

"Nothing. But, I'm a smart guy. I went to college for a long time."

"And I didn't?"

"Right. Anyway, we can figure this out together."

They stared at each other for a moment. Samantha loved looking at him, but she'd never tell him that. He had those rugged, chiseled features that women read about in romance novels. His hair was thick yet wispy in spots. And she loved how, after dinner, he literally got a five o'clock shadow that she wanted to run her fingers across…

"I've got it!"

"What?" she asked, leaning across the table.

"Old Mister Downs is selling his legal practice. You can say that you're in negotiations with him to take it over. That way, it makes sense that you have to go back to Atlanta, but you have ties up here. Then, the whole thing falls apart and you end up stuck in the city until you can open your own practice up here."

"Who's old Mister Downs?"

"Oh, he's this ancient man who did my real estate closing. He's like a hundred and fifty years old and has hair growing out of his earlobes…"

"Stop!" Sam said, putting up her hand. "Or my steak might land right back on this plate."

"Yuck. Let's not do that. I watch dog's throw up all the time, but people? No thank you."

"Can you please focus?" Sam asked with a giggle.

"Sorry. I think I had too much of that wine. Is that city wine? I'm used to moonshine up in these parts."

"You are not!" Sam laughed so hard that she almost spilled her own glass of wine.

"Maybe we need to work off this giddiness."

"And how shall we do that?"

"Well, we shall dance, Miss Ryan," he said, standing up and pulling her hand.

"Tucker, there's no music."

"We can fix that," he said, removing his phone from his pocket. Within seconds, he was playing what seemed to be a station of love songs. Sam felt like a nervous schoolgirl about to go on her first date.

"Are you sure we should do this?" she asked softly as he pulled her closer and danced her over to the window overlooking the river.

"Dancing? It's so scandalous," he whispered against her ear.

"Tucker, I thought we agreed…" she was quickly losing her ability to think critically. A mixture of attraction and wine had taken over her brain.

"Relax, Sam. Just be here with me right now. After all, I'm your pretend fiancé."

She smiled as she looked up at him. "Fine."

He twirled her around and they swayed back and forth to the music. At first, it was funny and then the movements got slower. And then she realized he was holding her that way again. The way that made her want to curl up in a ball like a kitten.

Being with Tucker just felt right, but the logic

made no sense. She couldn't just uproot her life to drool over a man she'd only just met. But sometimes it felt like she'd known him forever. And every time he held her, it felt like she needed him more than her next breath.

Maybe it was just puppy love, the kind you have in middle school when the cutest boy in the class smiles at you across the room. But this felt like way more than that.

As they moved to the music, she realized how well their bodies fit together. She was considered on the taller side for a woman, but he still towered above her, allowing her to perfectly nuzzle her face just under his chin.

Maybe it was the wine, but she felt like she was melting into him. Like if she danced much longer against his body, she might just disappear altogether. Still, she danced.

"You know this is all going to be okay, right?" Tucker said, his lips partially pressed against the top of her head.

"I guess so."

He tilted her chin up and met her eyes. "Look, Sam, I know we aren't really engaged and this is all an act. But I care about you more than you know. I'm not going to let Clark get the better of you."

She smiled. "Thanks, Tucker. But you don't have to protect me."

"I want to protect you," he said softly. He leaned closer, but only kissed her forehead. She felt the absence of his lips on hers, but she understood. The more they gave in and kissed, the harder her leaving was going to be.

"Can we just keep dancing?" she asked softly. Without missing a beat, Tucker pulled her closer and she melted into him once more, allowing herself the illusion that she was living the life she really dreamed of.

CHAPTER 12

"So, how's Paris?" Samantha asked her sister. It had taken awhile to finally get a phone call from the new bride, a sign that the honeymoon was going well.

"Magical. Seriously."

"I bet."

"And how's Whiskey Ridge?" Katie asked with a giggle.

"The same. Magical," Sam responded, laughing. Although she really did feel like it was a pretty magical place lately.

Spending all of her time with Tucker, at least when he wasn't working, had become her new norm. She knew she was playing fast and loose with her heart at this point. There was no doubt that she had some strong feelings, and for some reason she'd just given up on trying to deny them. She was just enjoying the time they had together right now. Living in the moment had never been her strong suit.

"And how's Tucker and the whole fake engagement thing? Has anyone found out?"

Samantha sighed. "Clark didn't buy it at first..."

"Clark? What's he still doing there?"

"Oh, that's the lovely part. He's staying here indefinitely. So he's been watching us like a hawk and questioning my every move."

"What does Tucker think about all of this?"

Sam smiled to herself. "He's very protective, actually. He purposely calls Clark by the name Craig just to rile him up. And he passionately kisses me any time we see Clark coming. It's hysterical."

Katie was silent. "Wait. What? He kisses you?"

Sam swallowed hard and realized what she'd just said. "Well, yes. I mean, we're supposed to be engaged."

"Sam, it's me you're talking to. You said he's protective? What does that mean?"

"I mean he doesn't want Clark to get the upper hand with me."

"Sam, do you have feelings for Tucker?"

"What do you mean?" She was trying to deflect, a tactic she often broke apart when witnesses tried to use it in the courtroom.

"You know what I mean. Are you in love with Tucker?"

Sam paused and thought for a moment. Was she in love? All she knew was that she'd never felt quite like this before, but that was probably just lust, right? Not love.

"Sam? Are you still there?"

"Yeah. I'm here," she said softly.

"You love him?"

"I don't know." There, she'd said it out loud now. No taking it back.

"Does he love you too?"

"I don't know."

"You haven't told him?"

"No. And I'm not going to."

"What? Why not?"

"Because it's ridiculous. First of all, I just met him! Two people cannot fall in love that quickly."

"Um, that is totally untrue. When I first met Rick, it was like a lightning bolt for both of us. By the third week, he started talking about marriage. When you know, you just know."

"We can't be together, Katie. You know that."

"No. What I know is that you're choosing not to allow yourself to experience real love, Sam."

"So what am I supposed to do? Pick up my whole life for a man I just met, move to a town that has one traffic light and start all over, leaving my successful career in the dust?"

Katie sighed. "No, sis. You choose whether you want to pick up your life for you. Not for some guy. For you. What do you really want? The fast paced, non-stop city life of a busy attorney or the possibility of happily ever after?"

"I don't know."

"Well, it sounds like you have a decision to make."

"I don't even know how he feels about me, Katie."

"I think you do."

TUCKER REELED the line back in and sighed. "Okay, let's try this again. And this time, try not to throw it directly into the tree."

Sam giggled. "Maybe I was trying to catch a bird?"

"If you want a bird, I can buy a pack of chicken from the grocery store. But if you want fresh fish with my super secret rosemary marinade, we've got to pull some big ones out of this river today."

They stood on the shore of one of his friend's properties and cast their lines back in.

"I talked to Katie yesterday."

"Oh yeah? How's the honeymoon going so far?"

"Great. I wouldn't be surprised if I was back up here in about nine months waiting for my niece or nephew to be born."

Tucker smiled. "You think they're going right for the family thing?"

"Oh yes. Katie has always wanted a litter of kids."

Tucker leaned over and whispered, "I don't think you're supposed to call them a litter."

"Okay, a passel? A gaggle?"

"So, do you want kids?"

The question smacked her in the face. "What?"

"You heard me, Sam. It's incredibly quiet out here."

"I never really thought about it."

"Liar."

"Excuse me?"

"Every woman, and a lot of men, thinks about the question of having children."

"Fine. I have thought about it."

"And?"

"I guess I can admit that yes, I'd like to have a kid or two."

"Why is that so hard to admit?" he asked as he reeled in another empty line and then tossed it back into the water.

"I don't know. I guess I've always been so focused on my career that admitting I wanted a family too seemed…"

"Weak?"

"Yes."

Tucker reeled his line in and turned toward her. "Wanting a family isn't weak, Sam. It just means you realize you don't have to do this life alone. It means that you want something bigger than what a paycheck can provide. Nothing wrong with that." He turned and tossed his line again.

"So, what about you? Still want kids?"

"Absolutely."

"Why are you so sure?"

He smiled as he looked off into the distance. "Well, this for one thing."

"Fishing?"

"Yeah. I can't wait for the day I get to teach my son, or daughter, how to cast their line and reel in a big fish for dinner." The grin on his face gave her shivers up her spine.

"What if they're no good at it?" she asked with a chuckle, throwing her line out yet again.

"Well, I sure hope they're better at it than their mother!" he said laughing. Samantha froze in place.

"What did you say?" She dropped her pole to her side, the line laying flat across the water.

"I, uh... I mean, most women aren't the best at fishing.... So..."

"Tucker, were you referring to me?"

He looked up at the sky as if he was asking for some kind of heavenly assistance or maybe an immediate transport out of the awkward situation.

After a moment, he reeled his line in and put it on the ground before walking toward her. Sam had never been so nervous in her life, not even during her first court case.

"Look, I spoke out of turn. I know you aren't interested in me like that. And I know your life is in Atlanta, but..."

"But?" she said. He took her pole from her and laid it on the ground, even though the line was still floating on the water.

Tucker took her hands in his and looked at her. "I can't play this game anymore."

"Game?"

"I can pretend to be your fiance, Sam. But I can't pretend I don't wish it was true."

"What?" She was literally losing the ability to form words.

"I know we just met. And I know this makes no sense whatsoever. But I can't go on without telling you that I think I'm falling head over heels for you, Samantha Ryan."

"Tucker..."

"And you don't have to say you're falling for me. I don't expect that. I know you have obligations in Atlanta. I would never ask you to leave your life for my life up here. But I need you to know that I'm here. If you decide you want to pursue a future with me, I need you to know that I want that with every fiber of my being."

She stared at him, his words sinking in slower than they should have. What should she say? What did she want to say? What did she want in her life?

"I don't know what to say."

Tucker smiled, a sad expression on his face for a fleeting moment. "I think that says everything." He released her hands and started to turn, and then Samantha did something she never expected to do. She grabbed his arm, turned him back around and kissed him like her life depended on it.

When they finally broke apart for air, Tucker's face was flushed and confused.

"Wait. What did that mean?" he asked, a crooked grin playing on his face.

"It means I feel the same way, Tucker. I find myself wanting to spend every waking moment with you. And I don't know how to handle this. I don't know what to do…"

He brushed his thumb across her cheek. "You're falling for me too?"

"Yes, and it's irritating," she said, groaning. Tucker laughed.

"I can imagine. You never expected this to happen, huh?"

She crossed her arms and sighed. "Why'd you have to be such a good guy and ride in on your white horse to save me at the bar that night?"

Tucker sat down on a log overlooking the river and patted for her to join him. She sat and leaned against him.

"Honestly, I wracked my brain for a long time trying to figure out why I swooped in like I did that night. I've never done anything like that before, but there was something in your eyes. Something that made me want to protect you. And that feeling hasn't left yet, Sam." He continued staring out at the water as it rushed by.

"I was so grateful, but I had this love hate thing going on with you at the time."

"Love?"

"Just an expression. I didn't love you then at all," she said laughing. Then she froze. Oh no.

Tucker turned to her. "You love me now?"

"I didn't say that," she said, trying not to move like he wouldn't notice her sitting there.

"Sam?"

She tilted her head up at him and met his eyes. "Fine. Yes. I think I love you. Dang it!"

She stood up and walked a few feet away, but he followed her as he always did.

"I love you too," he whispered in her ear from behind as he slid his arms around her waist. She laid the back of her head against his chest.

"Tucker, this isn't good. I can't stay here. We both know that. And having a long distance relationship with my work schedule and your business... it just won't work."

He was quiet. "Do you think you'll ever want a different life, Sam?"

She pulled away and turned to him. "Do you think you'll ever want a different life, Tucker?"

He paused. "No."

"Well, what makes you think I will?"

"I don't know. I just get the feeling that you want more."

"More doesn't have to mean living in this quiet little town."

"I thought you were starting to like it here?" He looked pained, as if she was ripping the rug right out from under him.

"I do like it here, Tucker. But I'd be in fantasy world to think I could ever build a business and a life here. I can't just walk away and give up all that I've built these last few years. There are financial considerations…"

"Oh, well, I guess I know the priority now, right?" He turned and went back to grab his fishing pole and starting putting his gear away. Sam hadn't seen him this upset before.

"Tucker, come on. We both knew this wouldn't work. I mean, you knew that, right?"

"Then why kiss me like that?"

She sighed. "I don't know. It was just a moment. I felt compelled…"

"Well, thanks for the moment."

"Please don't be like this."

"Like what? Like I'm reliving my divorce all over

again, but this time with a woman I love more than my next breath?"

"Your divorce? You can't compare me to that woman!"

"Very similar situation, Sam."

"No, it's not. She was a self absorbed person who didn't care about how you felt. That's not what I'm doing, Tucker, and you know it. I have a life and a business. I can't just drop it. How is that fair to me? Why can't you just drop everything and move to the city? Work in an animal clinic downtown?"

"Because I'd be miserable."

"So I'm the only one who should be miserable then?"

He closed the space between them and put his hands on her cheeks. "You need to ask yourself what really makes you happy, Sam. What really fuels your soul. What makes you wake up in the morning with a smile on your face. If it's your business, then I can accept that. But if it's me, then please think about this. I want you in my life, but I can't get hurt like that all over again. I can't do it."

With that, he turned toward the truck, and Sam quietly followed behind him. Her life was a wreck.

CHAPTER 13

*S*am sat at the coffee shop, hoping to goodness she didn't see Clark or his peppy fiancee. She just didn't have it in her today. She hadn't spoken to Tucker in days, and Katie was due to arrive home in a couple of days. Then it would all be over.

Her brief love affair with Tucker.

Her down time.

Her peaceful little mountain excursion.

And she'd go back to her normal life. The pace would be hectic, no doubt. After missing so much work time, she dreaded sitting back behind her desk staring at contracts.

Samantha was taken aback at her own thoughts. She was dreading work?

It wasn't really the work itself she was dreading as much as not having the time outside of work to have fun, be in love, feel peaceful.

As she sat there thinking about her time in Whiskey Ridge, she realized that she would actually miss the place. The people. The peace.

When she thought about her apartment in the city, and even her personal chef, it made her feel anxious. Nervous. A little queasy.

"What is wrong with me?" she mumbled under her breath.

"What was that, ma'am?"

An older gentleman had been sitting at the table beside her the whole time, but she hadn't noticed him until now.

"Oh, nothing. I was just talking to myself," she said, smiling slightly before turning back to her drink.

"Sounds like you're having a rough day?"

It was obvious this man wasn't going to stop talking to her, so she turned to face him. He was old, very old. Maybe pushing his nineties. He had a fluffy white beard like Santa Claus, and wore those little round glasses at the tip of his nose. Maybe he was Santa.

"I'm fine, really. Just fretting over some work stuff."

"Oh? What kind of work do you do?"

"I'm an attorney. In Atlanta."

"Oh my. Atlanta? Haven't been there in years. Such a busy place."

"Yes, it is. Pretty fast paced."

"And how do you like your work?"

"I love my work."

"Why?"

Why did old people like to talk so much? Maybe it was because they had more time to chat being retired and all.

"I love helping people, I guess."

"Hmmm."

"Hmmm?"

"I hear the words, but darlin', it sure doesn't sound like you mean them."

She would normally be offended and put off by a strange man calling her "darlin'", but the way he'd said it wasn't like a put down. It was one of those requisite Southern terms of endearment.

Samantha thought for a moment before speaking. "Well, I'm kind of at a crossroads right now, I suppose."

The man slid his chair closer and took a sip of his coffee. "Why's that?"

"After being up here for a few weeks, I guess I find myself not wanting to leave, if that makes sense." Why was she telling this stranger her innermost thoughts?

"Oh yes. Whiskey Ridge does have a way of doing that, I'm afraid. So why are you going back to Atlanta then?"

"Well, my life is there."

"You have a husband?"

"No."

"Kids then?"

"Not yet."

"Then what's drawing you back there?"

"My business. It's thriving."

"But are *you* thriving, hon?" The way he looked at her was so caring and concerned, like he really wanted to help her. It almost made her tear up.

"No, I'm not. I'm exhausted most of the time when I'm back there. I want to be this superwoman, you know? I want to do it all."

"What made you want to be a lawyer?"

"I wanted to help those who couldn't help themselves. I wanted to make money too, of course. But lately the money doesn't…"

"Keep you warm at night?"

She smiled. "That's one way to put it."

"Listen, I might be older than dirt now, and I've certainly already pulled a ticket in God's waiting room, but I do like to think I know a thing or two about life. And what I know for sure is this. Money, and all that it can buy, will never be enough without true love in your life. When I asked if you had a husband and kids, well, your eyes almost started to water. And when I asked about your business, your face tightened with stress."

"You have a love like that?"

"Oh, I did. For almost sixty years. She passed a couple of years ago. And I can tell ya from experience that there will never be a time that you wished you'd worked another day. But there will be a time that you wish you'd spent even another minute with your true love."

Samantha's eyes watered. "So what do I do? I have to make a living."

"No, hon, you have to make a life."

SAMANTHA STOOD on the front porch and waved as her sister and Rick pulled up in the driveway. Katie was all smiles as she bounded out of the car and straight into her sister's arms.

"Oh my gosh! I have so much to tell you! And I brought souvenirs from every country for you!"

"Welcome home to both of you! Sophie is dying to see you."

They went inside as Rick unloaded the car. Katie grabbed her sister's shoulders.

"Okay, spill it. What happened with Tucker after we talked? I've been dying to know."

"We haven't spoken in days now."

Katie's face fell. "What?"

Samantha explained what happened at the river. Katie sighed and hugged her sister.

"I'm so sorry, Sammy. You guys will mend fences."

"I don't know. But I have to head back to Atlanta in the morning regardless."

"I'm going to miss you so much."

"Listen, I need to call Eileen. She left me three voicemails. Mind if I step out on the deck?"

"Sure. Go ahead."

Sam stepped outside and dialed her assistant's number.

"Hello?"

"Boss! Dang, you're a hard woman to track down lately. What gives?"

"I've just been a little busy late."

"With what? Berry picking? Horseshoes?"

"Very funny. What's up?"

TUCKER DIDN'T WANT to go to the house, but he'd realized that he still had a pair of Sam's boots in his truck after their river visit. He had to return them, especially since he knew she was leaving soon. Plus, if he was honest with himself, he needed to see her. Say goodbye. Maybe cling on to her pant leg and beg her to stay.

She was all he could think about. Visions of white picket fences had been dancing through his head for days. But he wasn't doing this again. He wasn't going to chase a woman who didn't want him or a family life. His heart couldn't take it.

As he drove up, he realized Katie and Rick were home, so he knocked on the door.

"Hey, Doctor Ellison," Katie said as she opened the door, a look of surprise on her face. Sam had obviously told her everything.

"Hey. How was the honeymoon?"

"Fantastic!"

"Good. Listen, I just needed to drop off some boots your sister left in my truck. Is she around?"

"Sure. She's out back. Rick and I will be in our room unpacking."

"Okay," he said, as he walked into the house. He saw her through the window, but she didn't see him. She was on the phone, and he knew he shouldn't have listened in, but he couldn't help himself.

"So they want to sign a deal with me to be their sole representation then? How much? Oh my gosh, Eileen, that's more than I make in a year now... Yeah, but the hours I'll have to put in... I mean forget a social life, right?"

Tucker's heart dropped. She was taking on even more work? It was obvious that she wasn't interested in the life he wanted.

"When is the expiration date of their offer? Well, Al would have to take on some of my caseload, and the rest would have to be split among the other associates. I mean it could be done... I know, I know, it's a great opportunity..."

Tucker wanted to run out of the house. How had he been so wrong about her? How had he let himself fall in love with an unavailable woman?

"I think I want to go with option one that we

discussed. I know, Eileen. It's a huge move and a big risk, but I feel like…"

Just then, Tucker dropped one of the boots, sending a loud noise straight from where he was standing right to Samantha's ears. She turned with a start and almost dropped her phone, her eyes wide.

"Tucker? How long have you been standing there?"

"Long enough."

"Eileen, let me call you back later, okay?" She ended the call and looked at him. "Were you eaves-dropping on my conversation?"

"I didn't want to interrupt."

"So that would be a yes?"

"I brought your boots," he said, walking out onto the deck.

"Don't dodge my question. Were you listening to my conversation, Tucker?"

"I may have heard part of it, but it was definitely enough."

"I don't think you understand…"

"Oh, I completely understand, Sam. I misread the situation between us and your feelings for me. I was just a convenient part of your plan to deceive Clark and Monica, and nothing more." He started to walk down the stairs, but she followed him.

"You're the one who came up with that plan, Tucker Ellison. Not me!"

He continued toward his truck. "Well, you sure went along with it. Gosh, how could I have been so stupid? The moment you got a chance at more money, you took it."

She caught up to him at his truck. "It is my career, Tucker. You wouldn't take an opportunity in your career if one came along?"

He turned and looked at her. She was so beautiful, and it made him want to grab her and kiss her again.

"I would never take an opportunity that would have taken me away from you, Sam. Simple as that. Good luck in Atlanta."

He didn't give her a moment to respond before climbing into his truck and driving away.

Tucker had regretted that moment for over three weeks now. From what Katie had told him, Samantha was already gone back to Atlanta. He couldn't believe he'd left things on such a bad note.

He'd seen Clark around town during that time, which made him cringe. He'd done his best to still keep her secret, still protect her, although he didn't know why.

She didn't want him. She didn't want the life he wanted. And that should have been okay. But it just wasn't. Nothing felt right or worthwhile anymore. Dogs and cats could only provide so much joy. He wanted Sam. He needed her.

He'd thought a few times about driving to Atlanta and begging her to come back, but he wasn't that guy. He wasn't going to pressure her into doing something she didn't really want.

Another part of him thought seriously about taking that leap of faith and moving to Atlanta to show her how much he loved her. But him being miserable would have made him a terrible partner for her. She deserved better.

So they were at a stalemate. Nothing had changed, and nothing ever would.

Maybe he'd see her again one day when she visited her sister. Maybe she'd sneak into town and sneak right back out, avoiding him and Clark both now.

"Can I help you?" the woman behind the counter asked. He was at old Mister Downs' office to sign some final papers before construction of his home was to start. The home he'd dreamed Sam would live in one day.

"I'm here to sign some papers on my house," Tucker said, his mood somber. If this was what depression felt like, he never wanted to feel it again.

"Name?"

"Tucker Ellison."

"Okay, hon. Let me go check and see if they're ready for you."

The woman walked through a door and he was left to his thoughts again. He'd been stuck in his thoughts for weeks now, trying in vain to come up with an answer. A solution. Some way to make this all better. There just wasn't a way.

"Okay, he will see you now. Third door on the left is the conference room."

Tucker walked down the hallway looking at how Mr. Downs had decorated over the years. It was pretty dated with wood paneled walls and a musty smell, but then again Mr. Downs was getting on up in years himself and probably wasn't interested in redecorating.

"Tucker, old boy! Nice to see you again," the old man said as he slapped Tucker on the arm with a thud. He had to be related to Santa Claus.

"Hey there, Mister Downs."

"Listen, my hip is acting up something awful today. Do you mind if I let my associate handle this while I go take a nice, long soak in the tub at my house?"

Tucker cringed inside at the imagery of Santa Claus in the bathtub. He struggled not to shudder visibly.

"Um, sure. I didn't actually know you had an associate."

"Oh, yes. She's a firecracker I met a few weeks back. Pretty girl, but don't tell her I said that. It's not politically correct to say these things in the work-place anymore, you know."

"I know."

"Ah, well, here's your file. Go ahead and take a look, and she'll be in shortly."

"Thanks," Tucker said, taking the file folder and sitting down at the long, wooden table. He stared at the words, his eyes blurry after a long day at work. He really just wanted to go home, eat a bag of chips and watch ridiculous TV for the rest of the night.

"Any questions?" he heard a voice say from the doorway. He looked up, believing his ears were deceiving him. Samantha was standing there, a smile on her face.

"Sam? What are you doing here?" He didn't dare move, afraid she was some kind of delusion, and he liked this particular delusion.

"I'm here to go over your paperwork," she said, sitting down at the end of the table next to him. "Now, this document states that…"

"Sam?" he repeated again.

"Yes?"

"Why are you here? Why aren't you in Atlanta?"

She looked at him as if she was confused. "Well, that would be because my life is here in Whiskey Ridge, Tucker. And my business is here."

"What?"

She put her hand over his. "Tucker, you misunderstood what you heard that day at Katie's."

"I don't get it…" He was truly confused and at a loss for words.

"I met Mister Downs a few weeks ago at the coffee shop. We had a nice talk, and he let me know that he was looking for someone to take over here."

"I know. I told you that, remember? We were going to use it to fool Clark."

"Well, I realized that I could take this place over and do great things with it. More than just real estate closings. People up here really need a good attorney, someone who can fight for their rights.

People in the city don't need me like these people do."

"And people in the city don't need you like I do," he said softly, taking both of her hands. "But what about the conversation I heard? You had some big offer?"

"I did. But before you walked up, I'd told Eileen that option one was buying this place and staying in Whiskey Ridge. And then she told me about that offer."

"But then you told her you wanted option one."

"Right. So, I put two of my associates in charge of my cases in Atlanta, and I'm in the process of selling my company there for a fat wad of cash." She grinned.

"And you're okay with that?"

"Absolutely. That money is going to allow me to redecorate this place and start a whole new business that feeds my soul."

"But Katie told me you were in Atlanta."

"I was for a short time. Just to tie up loose ends. I swore her to secrecy."

"I can't believe this. I thought you wanted to be in Atlanta."

She squeezed his hands. "I want to be wherever you are, Tucker Ellison."

"And you're sure? You won't regret it and then hate me?"

She stood up, pulling him with her. "I will never regret choosing you, Tucker."

He pulled her into a passionate kiss, opening his eyes at the end only to notice Mr. Downs standing in the hallway with a smile on his face.

Six Months Later

"To the left. Perfect!"

Samantha stood in Tucker's living room, her hands on her hips, as she watched him hang the last piece of artwork she'd picked out for him.

"And we're done!" Tucker said as he jumped down off the step ladder.

"It looks wonderful, Tucker. A perfect reflection of you," she said smiling.

"And you, I hope?"

"Yeah, I guess there's a little of me mixed in here," she said with a chuckle.

He pulled her close, his arms around her waist. "I can't wait for you to be my wife, Samantha Ryan."

He'd asked her to marry him just four weeks ago, and she'd said yes without hesitation. After all, he'd been her fake fiancé for over seven months now anyway.

"I can't wait either," she said, pressing her lips to his.

"Did you ever think we'd outlast Clark and Monica?" Tucker asked with a grin on his face.

"Now, Tucker, that's not nice," she said, struggling not to laugh. Clark and Monica had split up weeks before their wedding when she'd met someone else on a yoga retreat out West. Apparently, their chakras had aligned and she just had to be with this guy who called himself Moonbeam. It was an almost unbelievable story.

Clark had crawled back to whatever hole he came from, which made Sam happy that she could enjoy Whiskey Ridge once again without fear of running into him.

Clark's opinion didn't matter anymore anyway. She had the man of her dreams and a life she could've never imagined, and her turn to be the bride was coming up soon.

"Knock knock! I come bearing gifts!" Katie called from the foyer. She was holding a big bouquet of flowers. "These are for your dining table."

Tucker took the flowers and placed them carefully on the table.

"How did you carry these heavy things?" he asked.

"I propped them right here," she said laughing as she pointed to her large belly. She was only six months pregnant or so, but she was having twins. Being short made her look like she was ready to pop any day now. "Gotta run. Rick's waiting in the car for my doctor's appointment. Have to find out how much these little nuggets weigh now!"

With that, Katie scurried out the door. Well, as much as someone carrying two babies can scurry.

Samantha stood there and smiled.

"What are you smiling about?" Tucker asked, sliding his hands around her waist as she looked up at him.

"I'm smiling at how much my life has changed since I met this sarcastic, critical veterinarian a few months ago."

"Oh, that's right around the time I met this snotty attorney who just couldn't take a joke."

"Oh really?" she said, inching closer to his lips. "And what ended up happening to her?"

"Well, this knight in shining armor helped her live happily ever after."

She pressed her lips to his. "I like the sound of that."

"I do have one more question for you, Sam Ryan."

"And what's that, you hunky veterinarian?"

He smiled. "Can we get a puppy?"

To READ all of Rachel's books, visit store. RachelHannaAuthor.com.

Made in the USA
Middletown, DE
25 October 2024

63305338R00128